Story a Day

**for every day
of the year**

AUTUMN

The Rescuers stories in this book feature characters from the Disney film suggested by the books by Margery Sharp *The Rescuers* and *Miss Bianca*, published by Little, Brown & Company.

Walt Disney's
Story a Day

for every day
of the year

AUTUMN

GOLDEN PRESS · NEW YORK

Western Publishing Company, Inc.
Racine, Wisconsin

Contents

Introduction

Here's one of a fantastic new series of Walt Disney books that's guaranteed to make *every* day of the year extra special! There are four books in the series—one for spring, one for summer, one for autumn and one for winter. Each book contains a story for every day of the season, so if you read all four you will have a story a day all year round, including one for the special days, like Christmas Day. All the stories have been specially written for the series and feature favorite Disney characters in lots of exciting and entertaining new adventures. And if you like to laugh you'll even find jokes in the books too! The illustrations, like the stories, are brand new and are all in sparkling color.

For every child who can read these books will make a treasured gift, and toddlers will find that bedtime *every* night will be a special event, as they fall asleep listening to tales of Mickey, Donald, Goofy and their Disneyland friends.

Puppies and Puddles

Lady and the Tramp have a mischievous puppy called Scamp. They took him for a walk in the woods one day.

"Now, Scamp," said the Tramp. "It rained yesterday, and there are muddy puddles about, so be careful where you walk."

Scamp wagged his tail in agreement, but he was so excited that he forgot about his promise, and when he saw a big, muddy puddle he leaped straight into it—SPLASH! Muddy drops flew into the air, and landed all over Lady.

"Oh, Scamp," sighed Lady. "Now I shall have to have a bath when I get home, to wash off the mud. You *are* a trouble and a worry to me."

Scamp said he was sorry and wouldn't do it again, but the next puddle he saw was so big and interesting that Scamp just couldn't help jumping into it—SPLASH! Poor Tramp was spattered with muddy water.

"Oh, Scamp," grumbled the Tramp. "You make such a lot of work for us. Why can't you be a good pup instead of being so mischievous?"

Suddenly, Lady heard a distant barking. She pricked up her ears.

Professor von Drake: "Let's talk about the grizzly bear. Does anyone know if we get fur from him?"
Huey: "I'd get as fur from him as possible."

"Why, I do believe it's our friend Perdita, the dalmatian. I heard a deeper bark, too. That must be Pongo."

Sure enough, Perdita and Pongo appeared after a
while. Behind them came fifteen jolly spotted pups.
Suddenly, one of them, called Patch, saw a puddle.

"Ooh, lovely, wet, sloshy mud!" he chuckled.

Then in he jumped—SPLASH! The other puppies
thought it looked like such fun that they all found
nearby puddles to jump into, too. Fifteen showers of
muddy water were soon flying into the air to soak poor
Perdita and Pongo! While Perdita and Pongo were
grumbling at their mischievous puppies, Lady and the
Tramp walked away, smiling.

"Come on, Scamp," the Tramp said. "Perhaps having
just one mischievous puppy isn't so bad after all. You
can't make as much mess as fifteen mischievous puppies.
I'm sure Perdita and Pongo love all their puppies very
much—but, all the same, I'm glad we only have one little
Scamp to worry about."

Scamp trotted after Lady and the Tramp.

"I think they've forgiven me for the splashes," he
thought.

Scamp couldn't quite understand why, but he was very
pleased that Lady and the Tramp weren't cross with him
any more!

9

Pinocchio's Blackberries

Pinocchio and his friend, Jiminy Cricket, had come to the woods to look for blackberries. Pinocchio had brought a bowl to fill. Yesterday, Geppetto had shown him a bush full of ripe blackberries, so Pinocchio knew where to start work.

"Geppetto said he would serve the blackberries with cream and sugar for our party," said Pinocchio.

Jiminy could only reach the lower blackberries, but Pinocchio could reach up really quite high. They put the bowl on the ground so that they could both put their fruit into it, and they kept a big leaf over it to keep the birds away. At last the bowl was full, but Pinocchio had seen one last blackberry that he wanted to pick. It looked juicy, but it was high on the bush—really too high for Pinocchio, but he was determined to reach it. He stretched his arm as far as he could. Then up on tip toe he stood. At last he had hold of the blackberry.

"Hurray!" shouted Pinocchio, stepping back.

"Don't step on our blackberries!" cried Jiminy.

Pinocchio tried not to step back and, in doing so, he wobbled and began to topple.

"Look out!" gasped Jiminy, trying to pull the heavy bowl back, out of Pinocchio's way, but it was no use.

With a horrid squelching sound Pinocchio fell backwards into the bowl of blackberries!

"Oh, Pinocchio—you've squashed our berries!" wailed Jiminy. But there wasn't enough time to search for another bush.

"We'll just have to take this dreadful mess home. At least Geppetto will know that we did what we were told and picked some blackberries. But he will be sorry that he can't eat any, after all," sighed Pinocchio.

Geppetto was sorry when he saw the squashed blackberries.

"But there's no need to throw them away," he said.

He carried the bowl into the kitchen. Then, to Pinocchio's and Jiminy's surprise, he set to work with a wooden spoon pushing the blackberries through a sieve, and the thick juice from the blackberries ran through into a dish.

Geppetto said: "We'll have ice cream with it instead of cream. The squashed blackberries have made a lovely blackberry sauce—just right to pour over ice cream."

Geppetto poured the blackberry sauce over three dishes of ice cream, sprinkled sugar over the blackberry sauce, and they began their feast.

It was delicious—one of the best blackberry feasts the three friends had ever had!

Orville Saves a Swallow

Bernard and Bianca, the two mice, had found a poor, injured swallow. The swallow had damaged its wing, and it couldn't fly south for the winter with the other swallows.

"The poor dear thing!" said Bianca. "We must help, somehow. What about Orville the albatross? He is big and strong enough to carry the swallow on his back. He could fly with it to the warm south, where it could join all the other swallows."

Orville the albatross happened to be staying quite nearby at that time, so Bernard and Bianca were soon able to find him and tell him about the poor swallow. Orville agreed to help, and Bernard and Bianca lifted the swallow gently on to his back. Bianca had bound the swallow's wing with bandages, to help it heal.

"Your wing should be better in a few weeks," Bianca told the swallow. "Enjoy your journey."

"Thank you so much, Bernard and Bianca," said the swallow. "Good-bye."

Pinocchio: "Why does the Mayor wear red suspenders?"
Geppetto: "To keep his trousers up, of course!"

After a great deal of running, wing-flapping, running, puffing, panting, and more wing-flapping and running, the albatross at last managed to get himself off the ground. Once in the air, his huge wings were soon carrying him high over the rooftops, over trees and fields. Then, as they flew over the sea, the swallow said:

"I'm very grateful to you, Orville."

"I have my uses, don't I!" said Orville, proudly.

By the time they reached the warm land where the swallow was to spend the winter, Orville and the swallow were great friends.

"I think I'll stay here for a while with you and the other swallows," said Orville. "I feel like a nice holiday in the sun."

Orville certainly deserved that, didn't he!

Boastful Toad

4

September

At the end of the summer Mr. Toad took his boat out of the water, and then he painted it. Now the paint was dry, and Toad asked Ratty and Mole to help him put it away in his boat-shed for the winter. It was a sad occasion for Toad. He loved his boat dearly. A huge tear trickled down his fat cheek.

"Never mind, Toad, old chap!" comforted Mole. "The spring will be here before you know it. You'll soon be sailing again."

"Dear old Mole, you're right, of course," said Toad.

At last, the boat was put safely away, and the three friends began to make their way to Toad Hall, where they were to have a party. Ratty and Mole did not look sad at all. The fact is, they were secretly rather glad to see Toad's boat put away for a while! They had heard nothing all summer but Toad going on and on about his famous boat being the biggest and best in the land, and how it could go faster than any other, and beat all the other boats in any race.

"Just think how peaceful the autumn and winter will be without hearing Toad boasting about his boat!" whispered Ratty to Mole.

Just at that moment Toad spotted a buckeye tree.

"I wonder if there are any buckeyes under the tree," said Toad.

He hunted on the grass, and there he found a real *beauty*!

"Why, it's the biggest buckeye in all the land," boasted Toad. "I'll win all the prizes with this giant. See how shiny and strong it is. . . ."

"Oh dear!" sighed Mole to Ratty. "Here we go again! We might have known Toad would find something else to boast about. Now we shall hear nothing all autumn except Toad going on about his famous buckeye!"

That Toad—he will never change, will he?

Mowgli's Coconut

Mowgli had found a coconut, and he wanted to crack open the shell so that he could eat the crunchy coconut inside. He decided that the best way to do it was to hurl it through the air and hope that it would crack open as it landed on the ground. Mowgli did hurl it, as hard as he could—WHEEEEEEEEE, it whizzed through the air! Then—BONK, it landed somewhere. Mowgli ran through the jungle, wondering just where his coconut had fallen. Then he heard a gruff, cross voice:

"Are you, by any chance, looking for this?"

It was Baloo, the big bear, who is Mowgli's friend.

"Yes, that's my coconut," said Mowgli.

"Then you might watch where you are throwing it next time," sniffed Baloo, and he walked away, limping slightly.

"Poor Baloo!" sighed Mowgli. "The coconut must have landed on his foot, and now he's upset with me."

Suddenly, there was a very loud thundering noise. It sounded to Mowgli as if all the trees in the forest were falling down! It was really Colonel Hathi, who was patrolling his elephants. They came marching past Mowgli, and thundered on through the jungle.

When they had gone, Mowgli looked around for his coconut. At last, he found it! The shell had been well and truly cracked open!

"One of the elephants must have trodden on it!" Mowgli cheered. "It's been broken into pieces which are just the right size for me to eat!"

"And me!" called Baloo, who had heard Mowgli's cheer, and come hurrying back.

Mowgli shared the pieces of coconut with the big bear, and soon they were the best of friends again.

15

Little Hiawatha's Canoe

Little Hiawatha has a canoe of his very own. It was given to him by his father, the Indian chief, and Little Hiawatha is very proud of it. As soon as he learned how to swim, his father allowed him to take his canoe on a shallow lake, and paddle it about all by himself, while his father watched from the shore. Little Hiawatha enjoyed this very much indeed, but sometimes he couldn't help feeling rather lonely.

"I do wish that some of the young Indian braves had canoes, too," said Little Hiawatha to his father, one day. "Then they could come canoeing with me."

The Indian chief thought for a while, and then he told Little Hiawatha that as it was tree-felling time he would allow the young Indian braves to have a tree trunk each, to use as a canoe.

"What a splendid idea, Father," said Little Hiawatha. "We'll ask the beavers to hollow out the tree trunks with their sharp teeth."

The beavers were soon at work, and the young braves were delighted with their tree-trunk canoes.

The Mad Hatter: "Which side of a tea-pot should the spout be?"
The March Hare: "The outside!"

"Let's all go canoeing now," said Little Hiawatha, when the new canoes were ready.

Little Hiawatha carried his canoe to the shallow lake, and the young braves carried their tree-trunk canoes. Soon they were all having fun together on the water.

The Indian chief watched them, feeling very glad that his little son now had lots of friends to keep him company.

Where is Figaro?

One day, Pinocchio was very worried.

"Where is Figaro, Daddy?" he asked Geppetto.

"I don't know," said Geppetto, to his little wooden puppet come-to-life. "I haven't seen him all day."

Figaro is their pet cat, and they couldn't bear to think that he might be lost. They searched the house for him, but he was nowhere to be seen.

"He must have gone out somewhere for the day," said Geppetto. "Let's get on with one of our jobs, and he will probably turn up, just when we aren't thinking about him."

Pinocchio doesn't like work very much, and he sighed when Geppetto said:

"All the garden tools must be cleaned and dried, and put away in the toolshed for the winter. We'll do it together."

"You must do as you are told, Pinocchio," said Pinocchio's little friend, Jiminy Cricket.

Pinocchio and Geppetto went out into the garden, and collected up all Geppetto's tools. They cleaned and dried them.

"Now make sure the toolshed is tidy, so that we can

Merlin: "My dog has no nose."
Mad Madam Mim: "How does he smell!"
Merlin: "Terrible!"

put the tools away in there," said Geppetto.

Pinocchio grumbled all the way to the toolshed at the bottom of the garden, but Jiminy Cricket told him he must do as he was told. Pinocchio opened the toolshed door, and then what a surprise he had! There, lying on a pile of sacks, was Figaro, who was looking very pleased with himself at having found such a warm, dry place to spend the day!

"Daddy! Daddy! I've found Figaro!" cheered Pinocchio.

"There! Didn't I tell you he would turn up when we weren't even thinking about him!" said Geppetto.

"There! Aren't you glad you did as you were told, Pinocchio, and helped Geppetto!" said Jiminy Cricket. "If you had been disobedient you wouldn't have found Figaro."

Pinocchio was pleased he had helped, and very, very pleased that he had found dear Figaro!

Dopey's Mistake

Minnie: "My tire has a puncture."
Daisy: "How did it happen?"
Minnie: "There was a fork in the road."

Snow White had made a big meat pie for supper. "The seven dwarfs will enjoy this," she said, as she put it into the oven. "I'll fetch some crunchy apples from the orchard, then we can each eat one after the pie."

Snow White decided to ask one of the dwarfs to fetch the apples for her, and she chose Dopey because he likes to be helpful when he can, and he isn't often asked to do useful things. Dopey set off to the orchard with a basket, and stopped at the first tree he came to. He rested his ladder against it, and had soon picked eight apples. Back went Dopey to Snow White's kitchen. She wasn't there, so he decided to taste one of the apples.

"UGH!" he gasped. "It's HORRID!"

Snow White came into the kitchen just then.

"Oh, Dopey," she said. "Those big green apples are **cooking** apples—not *eating* apples. You should have picked the little red ones."

Poor Dopey!

"Now all the other dwarfs will laugh at me," he sighed. "They often say I do everything wrong, and now I've picked the wrong apples! Oh dear!"

But Snow White told him not to worry, and said that the other dwarfs would never know that Dopey had picked the wrong apples.

"We'll cook these first, before we eat them," she said. "I'll bake them—that's one of the nicest things to do with cooking apples."

Dopey watched as Snow White washed the apples, and, using a special tool, took out the cores. She put the apples into a dish with butter and brown sugar, and put the dish into the oven with the pie.

At lunch time, when the meat pie had been eaten, Snow White took the baked apples from the oven, and gave one to herself and one to each dwarf. Inside the skins the fruit was fluffy, white and soft, and the butter and sugar had made a lovely, syrupy sauce to sweeten the apples. Snow White had made custard and cream to go with them.

"This is the nicest pudding we've ever had!" said Happy, between mouthfuls. "You have cooked the apples beautifully, Snow White."

"And Dopey picked them for me beautifully, didn't you, Dopey!" smiled Snow White.

Dopey looked pleased and proud. He took another mouthful of apple, and gave Snow White a secret wink!

Donald Duck's Car

Donald Duck's grandfather had given Donald his old car.

"I shall buy a new, modern one," said Grandfather. "I've had this one since I first began to drive, and now I want a change."

Donald was thrilled! The very old car was just what he wanted! You see, a special event was to take place that month. It was called the Veteran Car Rally.

"Lots of very old cars are going to be driven from Burbank to San Diego," Donald told Daisy Duck. "If I manage to drive this old car all the way to San Diego, lots of folks will be waiting there to cheer me."

"In that case," said Daisy, "the car must look shiny and clean. We'll work on it now, and ask our friends to help."

It wasn't long before Mickey and Minnie Mouse, Pluto and Goofy were all working on the car with Donald and Daisy. Minnie polished the mirrors, and Daisy cleaned the windshield. Donald checked the tires, and Mickey washed the car body and mudguards. Pluto fetched buckets of clean water, and when the car was dry, Goofy did the polishing.

On the morning of the Veteran Car Rally Donald set off, feeling proud of his clean, shiny old car. He was upset when it began to rain, for he knew that the polish would be washed away, leaving the paintwork dull. At last the rain stopped, but then an old car, also in the rally, went speeding by Donald, and splattered his car with mud. Donald didn't worry about it too much as he was only thinking about reaching San Diego before the rally finished. When, finally, he did reach San Diego, lots of folks were there to cheer him. Among them were Minnie, Mickey, Daisy, Pluto and Goofy. They had all come to San Diego earlier that day on the bus, so as to see the cars arriving. They had enjoyed themselves—until the moment when they saw Donald's muddy, splattered car.

"All our hard work for nothing!" sighed Daisy. "Why did we bother to make it look nice?"

Donald's friends, however, didn't have time to be sad for long, for Donald invited them all to a special dance held that evening in a big hotel. It was a dance for all the drivers who had managed to reach San Diego in their old cars. It was a very grand affair.

"I'm glad we cleaned your car after all," Daisy told Donald, "for if we hadn't been kind to you, we might not have been here to enjoy this splendid evening!"

23

Wonderland Dancing

Grumpy: "Ouch! A crab just bit my toe!"
Happy: "Which one?"
Grumpy: "How do I know? All crabs look alike!"

The Walrus and the Carpenter wanted to dance on the shore.

"Will you join the dance?" the Walrus asked Alice, in a friendly way.

"No, thank you," said Alice. "I don't like dancing without music. It's not easy to dance without music, you know."

"Tut! What a difficult child you are!" sighed the Walrus.

"If I sing," the Carpenter asked Alice, "would that help?"

"No, it wouldn't!" said Alice, at once. "You make a dreadful noise when you sing. I've heard you. I said I wanted to dance to music—not to a dreadful noise."

Just then the Walrus noticed Tweedledum and Tweedledee, who were coming along the beach together.

"We've been collecting driftwood, to use as firewood," said Tweedledum.

He was carrying two large logs, and Tweedledee had found two thin branches.

Now Alice knew what to do! She told Tweedledum and Tweedledee how they could help.

"Put the hollow logs on the sand, Tweedledum," said Alice. "Now, Tweedledee—you give one of your sticks to Tweedledum. Both of you bang a hollow log with a stick, and if you really think about what you are doing—you should be able to make some sort of tune for us to dance to."

Tweedledum and Tweedledee did as Alice had told them. It was a funny bonkity-bonk, plinkity-plonk sort of tune that they made, but it sounded better than the Carpenter's singing anyway, thought Alice.

"Now we can do a bonkity-bonk, plinkity-plonk sort of dance," said the Walrus, happily. "Come along, Carpenter and Alice."

The Carpenter and Alice joined the Walrus in his funny dance along the shore.

Well, it wasn't the sort of dancing Alice usually did, but then everything is slightly different and strange in Wonderland, isn't it?

Bongo Reaches the Blackberries

Piglet: "Does your watch tell the time?"
Tigger: "No, you have to look at it!"

The three little pigs wanted a blackberry pie for their lunch.

"I'll make the pastry," said Practical Pig. "You two go into the garden and pick the blackberries."

Fifer and Fiddler Pig went into the garden with their basket, but when they reached the blackberry bush they remembered that they had picked all the low hanging blackberries a few days ago.

"There are some nice ones left up there," said Fifer, pointing towards the top of the bush, "but how are we little pigs going to reach them?"

Fifer and Fiddler were gazing at the bush in a puzzled way, when they heard a voice coming from the garden gate.

Fifer and Fiddler looked towards the gate, and saw a little bear standing outside. He wore a smart hat and a jacket, and he was balancing on a little one-wheeled cycle.

"I'm Bongo the bear," he said. "I am on vacation in this area. I was passing, and I saw that you seem to be in trouble. I wonder if I may help you?"

Fifer and Fiddler explained about the blackberries, and then Bongo did a surprising thing! He climbed up on the garden fence, taking his one-wheeled cycle with him. He balanced the cycle on the top of the fence, climbed on to the saddle of his cycle, and began to pedal along the top edge of the fence!

"Don't worry. I won't fall!" called Bongo. "I used to be a famous high-wire artist at a circus, you see."

Bongo kept cycling until he was level with the top of the blackberry bush. From there, he reached out and picked lots of large, juicy blackberries. He tossed them down to Fifer and Fiddler, who caught them, and put them in their basket. Fifer and Fiddler were delighted! Fifer took the blackberries indoors to Practical Pig, and Fiddler asked Bongo to come down from the fence and join them in their blackberry-pie lunch.

Bongo did join the three little pigs, of course, and while they ate he told them all sorts of exciting stories about his life in the circus.

27

The Potato Zoo

Donald Duck had grown lots of potatoes in his garden, and it was now time to harvest them.

"We must dig them all up out of the ground, and put them into sacks to store for the winter," said Donald to Daisy.

Daisy Duck came to help Donald, and so did Donald's three little nephews, Huey, Dewey and Louie. Donald and Daisy worked very hard with their digging and sack-filling, but those cheeky young nephews just played around. They climbed into the empty potato sacks. Then they started throwing dirt about. Donald was very cross with them.

"How can Daisy and I get on with our work when we've got to stop all the time to keep you three in order?" complained Donald.

Then Daisy said, "I know how we can keep Huey, Dewey and Louie happy and out of mischief."

Some of the potatoes had been broken by the spades, and some of them were very misshapen. Donald didn't want to keep these, so Daisy gave them to Huey, Dewey and Louie.

"You can use them to make funny animals," said Daisy. "Use twigs for their legs, arms, tails and ears."

The three young ducks thought that was a splendid plan. The strange shapes made all sorts of funny animals, and they looked very fine with their twig arms, legs, ears and tails.

"We're making a potato zoo!" cheered Huey in delight.

Donald and Daisy were able to get on with their potato harvesting, while Huey, Dewey and Louie played very happily indeed.

Pinocchio's Useful Box

13
September

Geppetto is a kindly man who makes things to please his friends. He once made Pinocchio, the puppet, from wood. Pinocchio came to life, and he sometimes gets in mischief.

One day Jiminy asked Pinocchio:

"Why don't you be good, like Geppetto, and make something to please somebody?"

Pinocchio thought that was a good idea. He helped himself to some of Geppetto's wood, and set to work with hammer and nails. When, at last, he had finished, he had made a sort of square-shaped box that wasn't quite a square.

"What is it?" asked Jiminy.

"It could be a dollhouse for a girl," suggested Pinocchio, "or a garage for a boy. Geppetto makes toys for children, so he will know who would like to play with it."

When Geppetto saw Pinocchio's work, however, he said:

"I don't think it's the right shape for a dollhouse or a garage. I see I shall have to give you woodwork lessons."

Pinocchio was sad to think that his work wasn't good enough to please a child. For once, he had tried to be helpful—but no good had come of it.

Jiminy felt sorry for his friend, and he thought of a way to help. He remembered meeting a hedgehog that morning, and the hedgehog had been looking for somewhere to sleep for the winter.

"I need something roomy and dry, where I can put dry grass and leaves," the hedgehog had said.

Jiminy had not then been able to help, but now he knew the answer. He told Pinocchio to bring his wooden box outside for the hedgehog.

The hedgehog was delighted, and so was Pinocchio, who cheered: "I have made something useful, and it has pleased someone!"

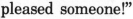

29

Toad's Hot Air Balloon

Mr. Toad had something new to show to his friends, Ratty and Mole.

"It's very special indeed," he told the puzzled pair, as he led them to Toad Hall. "I bought it yesterday."

As they arrived at Toad's huge garden, Toad pointed to an enormous hot air balloon which lay collapsed on the grass. It was attached to a basket.

"Toad obviously means to go traveling in a hot air balloon!" gasped Ratty, in alarm.

He and Mole watched as several balloon enthusiasts (hired by Toad) inflated the huge balloon. Then Toad climbed into the basket, and told Ratty and Mole to follow him.

"Come on, you two," insisted Toad. "We three are going on a balloon trip."

Ratty and Mole were rather nervous, but Toad would not let them refuse. The balloon enthusiasts told Toad just what he had to do, and they waved good-bye. As soon as the balloon was full of enough hot air it began rising—higher and higher it went. Toad switched off his special heater every now and then, so that the balloon

Queen of Hearts: "Do you file your nails?"
Alice: "No, I cut them off and throw them away!"

remained where it was, hovering. The basket below it was just level with the tops of the trees in Toad's garden.

Ratty and Mole were very puzzled, and they were even more puzzled when Toad leaned out of the basket and began picking buckeyes from the top of a very tall buckeye tree! Toad wore gloves, so that he would not prick his hands.

"The best buckeyes are always at the tops of the highest trees," said Toad. "Now I shall have the finest collection of buckeyes for miles around. As soon as I have enough buckeyes we'll go down to the ground again."

"Do you mean to say," gasped Ratty, "that you went to all the trouble of buying an expensive hot air balloon simply so that you could pick some high-up buckeyes?"

"What a way to set about buckeye-picking!" sighed Mole to Ratty.

It certainly was a surprising thing to do—even for Toad!

A Very Strange Tea Party

15 September

Alice was on her way to the Mad Hatter's garden for one of his tea parties. She didn't really want to go, because his tea parties were such strange affairs.

"But I wouldn't want to upset the Mad Hatter, so I must go," Alice told herself.

When Alice arrived at the garden, the Mad Hatter was already seated at the table, beside the March Hare.

"Where's the Dormouse?" asked Alice. "He's hiding in the teapot again, I suppose. Yes—out you come, Dormouse, and enjoy your tea."

Alice began to eat a sandwich—the oddest sandwich she had ever had! There were slices of cheese on the outside, and a piece of bread in the middle! But Alice didn't have time to say anything about it, because, at that moment, a large raindrop landed on her nose. Then more raindrops began pattering down onto the cups and plates. The wind began to blow, too, and Alice felt very cold. The Dormouse was shivering, and so was the March Hare. Alice was just about to say she thought they ought to go indoors, when the Mad Hatter suddenly ran into the house, and came out again, with his arms full.

"I had these things ready in case the weather changed," he said.

The Mad Hatter handed Alice a floppy sou'wester to keep the rain off her head, a big scarf to keep her neck warm, gloves, and a shawl to put over her shoulders. He gave the March Hare a warm hat, a thick pullover and mittens. He popped the Dormouse into a knitted tea cozy. The funny Mad Hatter had warm clothes for himself, too, and he put a big umbrella, on its side, at each end of the table to keep the wind and rain off the food.

"Well, really!" said Alice. "Wouldn't it have been simpler to take the table and tea things indoors out of the wind and rain?"

The Mad Hatter hadn't thought about that! He certainly is a very *mad* Mad Hatter, isn't he?

Seeds, Sneezes and Songs

It was a windy day, and the forest air seemed to be full of dandelion seeds. Every time Sneezy the dwarf stepped outside the house he sneezed:

"AAAAAAAA-TISH-OOOOOOO!"

"Sneezy, dear, I think you ought to stay indoors today," said Snow White.

"But, Snow White," sighed Sneezy, "I particularly want to go outside today. You see, the forest birds are about to fly south for the winter, and I want to listen to them singing their goodbye songs. They always sing to the forest folk before they set off on their journey. Doc, Happy, Sleepy, Bashful, Grumpy and Dopey are going to listen to the birds."

"But Sneezy, if you go outside, the dandelion seeds will make you sneeze, and the forest folk won't be able to hear the birds. They'll only hear you sneezing."

Sneezy had to agree that Snow White was right. Then he saw Snow White whispering to the other dwarfs, and they hurried away, smiling.

After a while, Doc, Happy, Sleepy, Bashful, Grumpy and Dopey returned to the house, bringing with them all the forest birds who were about to fly south.

"The birds are coming *indoors* to sing to you, Sneezy," explained Snow White. "Now you won't have to go outside to listen to them, and you won't have to go near all those dandelion seeds."

It was rather a crush by the time Snow White, the Seven Dwarfs *and* all the birds had managed to get themselves inside the house. But there was room enough for the birds to sing, and for the others to enjoy listening. The goodbye songs were very sweet, and Sneezy was so glad he hadn't had to miss them.

33

The Ugly Sisters' Treasure Hunt

Fiddler Pig: "Look, I've told you eighty-three billion times not to exaggerate!"

Young Cinderella had two Ugly Sisters, who made her do all the work in the house. They weren't a bit kind to her, and poor Cinderella had to do the cooking, the cleaning, the mending, the shopping and the washing—all by herself.

Jaq and Gus and their little mouse friends, who lived at Cinderella's house, were very sorry for her.

One day the two Ugly Sisters thought of an extra job for Cinderella to do.

"She can dig the garden," said one Ugly Sister. "It ought to be dug over before the winter frosts come."

"Get to work, Cinders," they told her. "The tools are all in the toolshed."

"We must help Cinderella, we must!" said Jaq to Gus. "She has quite enough work to do in the house without seeing to the garden as well. The Ugly Sisters ought to do the garden themselves. They do nothing all day! I know how we can trick the Ugly Sisters! If they think that there is some *treasure* hidden in the garden, then they will dig for it themselves to stop Cinderella from finding it!"

"But how do we make the Ugly Sisters think that there is treasure hidden in the garden?" asked Gus.

"I'll draw a pretend treasure map," said Jaq, "and hide it in an old bottle in the garden."

Jaq drew a very clever map and hid it in a bottle at the front of the first flower bed, so that Cinderella would be sure to find it. She did find it, and the Ugly Sisters saw her looking at it.

"What's that? What's that?" demanded the Ugly Sisters.

They snatched the map from Cinderella, studied it and then looked at each other in an eager way. They snatched the tools from Cinderella and began digging at great speed. They told Cinderella to go indoors.

Cinderella was very glad to have a rest. Of course, the Ugly Sisters didn't find any treasure at all! They were very cross at having worked so hard for nothing, and they never did solve the mystery of the mysterious treasure map!

Uncle Scrooge's 'Brooms'

Donald Duck has an Uncle Scrooge, who is very stingy about spending money. He has lots and lots of money, but he won't spend *any* of it at all if he can help it.

When autumn came, one year, and Uncle Scrooge's garden was covered with leaves, he really should have bought himself a new broom, and set to work sweeping them away. Uncle Scrooge, however, was too stingy to spend money on a new broom. Instead, he went to the back of his garden, where a family of hedgehogs lived. They hadn't yet gone to sleep for the winter, and Uncle Scrooge made them all roll themselves up into balls, and then roll across his lawn. As they rolled, the dry leaves stuck onto their prickles. When they reached the other side of the lawn, Uncle Scrooge removed the leaves from their prickles, and put them into a pile. After several hedgehog rollings the lawn was free of leaves.

"Now the lawn looks nice, and I saved myself from having to spend money on a broom!" cheered Uncle Scrooge.

Alice: "Did you meet your mother at the station?" **Christopher Robin:** "Oh no, I've known her for years!"

"Mr. Scrooge!" cried the hedgehogs, just then. "We're hungry!"

Uncle Scrooge had to give them something to eat after they had done all his work for him, and he knew that they couldn't begin their winter sleep feeling hungry.

"All right. Come into the kitchen," he sighed. "You can only have milk and bread. Everything else is too expensive."

Milk and bread are just what hedgehogs like, of course, and they were so hungry and thirsty that they ate two whole loaves between them, and drank three pints of milk.

"Well!" sighed Uncle Scrooge, when the hedgehogs had gone back to their home. "Those hedgehogs have eaten and drunk so much and cost me so much that I might as well have bought a broom in the first place. What a mean old silly and a silly old meanie I have been!"

Clarabelle's Canary

Clarabelle the cow has a pet canary who lives in a cage by Clarabelle's window. He is happy there, and when he sees birds flying by the window outside, he doesn't feel sad, and long to be with them. You see, Clarabelle looks after him very well indeed. He has fresh water and seed every day. He is allowed to fly around the room every afternoon, and he has his own special little wheel, ladder, swing, bell and mirror to play with.

One day, however, when the little canary looked out at the wild birds, he did feel sad, for Clarabelle told him that the birds were flying to the warm South.

"They are going there to spend the winter months," explained Clarabelle.

"Oo, I do wish I could go to the warm South," thought the little bird. "Now that summer is over I'm beginning to feel very chilly. Perhaps I'll try and escape, this afternoon, when Clarabelle lets me out of my cage. Then I can fly off to the warm South with the wild birds."

Gus: "But what do we do if we see a big tiger?"
Jaq: "Just hope that the tiger doesn't see us!"

38

As soon as Clarabelle let him out of his cage, after lunch, the canary looked around for a way of escape. The trouble was that Clarabelle had shut all the windows before opening his cage door. There was no way out! The little bird felt miserable when, after supper, Clarabelle put him back in his cage, and he felt even colder than he had in the morning.

"Do you know, I think it's time to put on the *central heating*!" said Clarabelle. "I switched it off for the summer. Now, just you wait a moment, and something nice will happen."

Clarabelle turned on a switch in the cupboard under the stairs. The canary could hear the boiler working away, and the radiators began to make a bubbling sound. As the radiators grew warm, the room became warm, and the little yellow bird became warm.

"How lovely!" he thought, ruffling his feathers with pleasure. "I've no need to fly to the warm South now. I think the warm South has come to me instead!"

39

A Very Grand Parade

Along the road come some jolly Disney folk. Where do you think they are going?

Look—there's Mickey Mouse, looking very smart, and Minnie, too. Pluto is beside them, and Goofy behind them. Where do you think they can be going?

Now, here comes King Lion, followed by Winnie-the-Pooh and Tigger. There's Thumper, and Chip 'n' Dale, the chipmunks. Where *are* they all off to?

Next comes bad Captain Hook, followed by Brer Rabbit and Brer Fox. There's big Baloo, the bear, and funny Donald Duck. Where are they off to, we wonder.

After them come King Louie, Little John, Robin Hood and Prince John. And—oh, look—horrid Cruella de Vil, and some of the little dalmatian puppies she is always unable to capture. Where do you think they are all going?

Why, they are going to the LORD MAYOR'S SHOW! They are going to parade through the City of London, for all the girls and boys to see. The brand new Lord Mayor of London, himself, will be there, of course, in a very grand coach. Some of his helpers will be there too, and lots of smart soldiers and sailors. Several bands will be playing exciting music, and there will be colorful floats to see. Our Disney friends will feel very proud and happy as hundreds of children smile at them and wave. In fact, if you listen very carefully, you are sure to hear them saying that the day of this very special parade is their most exciting day ever!

Pleasant Pheasant Ride

Flora, Fauna and Merryweather, the three Fairy Godmothers, have been invited to a party at the palace of Sleeping Beauty and her Prince. They each had a beautiful gown to wear to the party. Flora's was a soft pink, Fauna's was blue, and Merryweather's was yellow and green. They felt very pleased with themselves as they stepped out of their front door when it was time to leave home for the party. But those three Godmothers did *not* feel pleased when they saw the huge muddy puddles all over the ground. It had been raining heavily, and the ground was very damp indeed!

"Oh dear!" sighed Flora. "Our lovely long dresses will be ruined! We shall arrive at the party splattered with water and mud!"

Fauna looked worried, but Merryweather was busy watching a beautiful bird fluttering down into the hedgerow nearby. It was a pheasant. That pheasant gave Merryweather an idea!

"I know!" she said, and she waved her magic wand and uttered a magic spell.

There was a bright flash of light, and suddenly on the path beside the three Godmothers appeared a HUGE pheasant! It was much bigger than the one Merryweather had seen a moment ago. It was much bigger than Flora, Fauna and Merryweather themselves! At first Flora and Fauna were rather frightened, but before they could run away Merryweather explained:

"This friendly giant pheasant will carry us on his strong back to the party! He will carry us over the mud and over the puddles, and we shall arrive at the party looking clean and tidy."

Sure enough, the pheasant was soon on his way, with the three Fairy Godmothers riding happily on its back.

"This is very pleasant—riding on a pheasant!" chuckled Merryweather. "Look—there's Sleeping Beauty's palace in the distance. I'm sure we're going to have a marvelous time at the party."

And, do you know, they *did*!

Roquefort's Cousin

Roquefort's mousehole is in a grand house in Paris. The house is beautifully furnished, and everywhere there are colorful, bright, cheerful, interesting and exciting things for Roquefort to see.

"I'm glad my mousehole is in such a splendid place," thought Roquefort, one morning. "I shall go out of my hole and look around the house as soon as I have finished breakfast. There's bound to be something new for me to look at. How glad I am that I am not like my cousin."

Roquefort's cousin lives in England. He is a church mouse, because he lives in a church.

"I shouldn't care to live in a church," thought Roquefort. "Churches are often big, dark and draughty. I don't suppose he has exciting things to see."

It was then that Roquefort decided to visit his mouse cousin.

"Perhaps I can persuade him to come to Paris," thought Roquefort. "I must brighten up his poor dull life."

Roquefort set off for England that very day. He managed to get himself rides on the backs of several trucks, and he stowed away on a ship. It was several weeks after Roquefort had first left Paris that he arrived

Huey: "Can you light a fire with two sticks, Unca Donald?"
Dewey: "He could if one of them was a match!"

42

at the big church, where he knew he would find his cousin. The mouse was thrilled to see Roquefort.

"I'm glad you've come today," he said. "Today is a special day, because lots of people are going to come and decorate the church for Harvest Festival."

The mouse explained that this was a special service in which everyone said 'thank-you' for the harvest. Folk soon began arriving, bringing apples, loaves of home-made bread, wheat, barley, pears, plums, nuts, berries and pots of homemade jam. These were arranged around the altar, and the rest of the church was decorated with flowers, grasses, leaves and plants. That evening the people came back in their best clothes, and the church was filled with the sounds of organ music and hymn singing.

"I see that a church mouse has an interesting life, after all," said Roquefort.

"Oh yes," squeaked his cousin. "At Christmas time, too, the church looks beautiful, and at Easter and Mother's Day, and there are always fresh flowers to see every week."

Roquefort didn't have to feel sorry for his church-mouse cousin any longer!

A Harvest Supper

Robin Hood's jolly friend, Friar Tuck, was busy planning a Harvest Supper. He had invited Robin to it as well as Maid Marian, Little John and Allan-a-Dale. He had made a high, wooden table especially for the occasion, and Marian had lent him one of her large white tablecloths. Friar Tuck had prepared lots of delicious homegrown fruit and vegetables, and he had made some of his special crusty bread.

At last, Friar Tuck's guests arrived and seated themselves around the table.

"Tuck in!" laughed Friar Tuck.

He and his guests were just about to begin their feast when they heard a noise—a crackling of dry twigs somewhere away in the forest.

"It may be our enemies!" said Robin. "Get ready to fight!"

Friar Tuck looked very sad.

"But, Robin, I'm so hungry. Fighting always takes such ages, and I'm all ready to enjoy our Harvest Supper NOW! Please let's hide, instead. There is room for us all under the table, and the long tablecloth will hide us from anybody's view."

Wicked Stepmother: "I've got a ladder (run) in my tights!"
Madame Bonfamille: "What do you want, a marble staircase!"

"Very well, Tuck!" laughed Robin. "Come on then, all of you—under the table! Bring the food and drink with you."

Robin, Friar Tuck, Little John, Maid Marian and Allan-a-Dale all clambered under the table, taking everything with them. It was like being inside a tent. They could not see out, because the tablecloth reached down to the ground, but they could hear voices!

The Sheriff of Nottingham, Prince John and Sir Hiss, the snake, had come looking for Robin and his friends, hoping to capture them.

"There's no one here," said the Sheriff, as he came into the clearing. "Just an empty table and chairs! They must have gone off somewhere to find food for their supper. Let's go and search the forest for them."

"Yessssss! Let'ssssssssssss!" hissed Sir Hiss.

"Off we toddle!" giggled Prince John.

The three of them hurried away, and did not return to the clearing again.

How Robin and his friends laughed! They came out from their hiding place, replaced the food and drink on the table, sat on their chairs and began their feast, still laughing about their funny adventure.

It was a very, very happy Harvest Supper!

45

Lovely, Lovely Mud

"Lovely, lovely mud!" chuckled the Lost Boys, as they played on a bank beside a shallow stream. They were making mud pies.

Meanwhile, Wendy, John, Michael and Peter Pan had been searching Never-Never Land for the Lost Boys.

"Now I know why they're called Lost Boys," laughed Michael. "It's because they're always getting lost!"

Wendy *didn't* laugh, however, when, at last, she found the Lost Boys—in the *mud*!

"They'll have to be washed, and so will their suits!" sighed Wendy. "You are naughty boys."

Now, all this time, SOMEONE was creeping along the stream below—very slowly, so as not to make a splashing sound. It was wicked Captain Hook, who is always trying to capture Peter Pan and his friends. Behind Captain Hook came Mr. Smee, one of his pirate crew.

"Stop, Smee!" whispered Captain Hook.

The Captain pointed to the bank above, where they could hear Wendy complaining.

"We'll creep up the bank and capture them!" chuckled Hook.

He stepped out of the stream, and started climbing up the bank on all fours. Halfway up, Smee, who was following him, gasped: "Just look at your clothes, Captain!"

The feather on Hook's hat had once been a soft

Uncle Scrooge: "Coffee without cream, please."
Edgar: "We're out of cream, sir. Will you have it without milk?"

46

pink—now it was muddy brown, and plastered down over one side of Hook's face. His face, too, was muddy, and mud was dripping from his moustache. His trousers, his red jacket and his frilly shirt were covered with mud, as well as his stockings and shoes. Hook has always been very proud of the way he dresses. Now he bent over the stream and looked at his reflection in the water. What a horrid surprise he had!

"*Oh my!*" he gasped. "I must return to the ship at once, and clean myself up, before my clothes are ruined. Smee, come and help me—on the double now!"

With a huge splash, Hook and Smee jumped back into the stream, and hurried away.

Peter, Wendy, John, Michael and the Lost Boys heard Smee gasp, and they peeped over the edge of the bank, to see the disappearing pirates.

"If it hadn't been for the mud," said Peter, "Hook would have climbed right up the bank and captured us!"

"As the mud has been helpful—can we go on playing with it?" asked the Lost Boys.

Wendy agreed.

"After all, they're having such fun," she said, "and I'll have to wash their suits now, anyway."

As Wendy walked away with Peter, John and Michael, they could hear the Lost Boys singing:

"Lovely, lovely mud!"

Pooh's Honey Jars

Winnie the Pooh looked at himself in the mirror. "Christopher Robin is right!" he sighed. "I ought to lose some weight. I like being a fat bear, but not *very* fat! Dieting is hard for me, because I love my food—especially lovely honey. Christopher Robin says I mustn't have any honey for a week, but I couldn't bear that! However, instead of eating *large* jars of honey, I shall eat *small* ones."

Pooh bought himself some small jars of honey. The small jars were made of glass—not like his big stone jars. Every day he finished up several of them, and as he still felt hungry he had several more! Silly Bear! Because he ate twice as many small jars, he was eating just as much honey as if he had had large jars! But he felt proud of himself, and as he was looking in the mirror one day, to see if he looked slimmer, there was a knock at his door. Outside stood Piglet, Tigger, Eeyore, Rabbit, Owl, Kanga and Roo—who were on their way to Christopher Robin's birthday party. Pooh had been invited, too,

so he joined the others. When they all arrived at the party, Christopher Robin said sadly:

"There has been a power cut! The storm last night brought down the cables that bring electricity to our house, so we cannot switch on the electric lights. It will be dark soon, and how can we have a party in the dark?"

"I have some night-lights," said Christopher Robin's Nanny.

Nanny kept some little candles, called night-lights, and she lit one each night for Christopher Robin to have in his room. He had a special holder to put his night-light in.

"But we've only one holder," said Christopher Robin. "It wouldn't be safe to use night-lights without holders."

Then Pooh remembered his little honey jars. They were just the size for night-lights, and there were lots of empty, clean ones at home. Pooh hurried to fetch his jars, and Nanny put a night-light in each one. She arranged the jars around the room and lit the night-lights. As it grew darker outside, the room seemed to grow brighter and cozier. Christopher and his guests enjoyed their candle-lit party.

"If my jars are going to be as useful as this," thought Pooh, "I'd better eat lots more honey, in case anyone else wants to borrow some jars."

What a lovely excuse for him to eat more honey!

Little Hiawatha's Headdress

Little Hiawatha wears a special Indian headdress. It is a single, large feather on a band, and Little Hiawatha has always been proud of it. One day, however, he decided that he wanted a bigger and a better headdress. In fact, he wanted one just like his daddy's. Now Little Hiawatha's daddy is an Indian chief and allowed to wear a full headdress with lots and lots and lots of feathers. Hiawatha tried on his daddy's headdress one day, while his daddy was asleep.

"I just must have one like it," said Little Hiawatha.

He left the Indian camp and hurried away into the wild country. He knew where to find some feathers. He went to the rocky land beneath the big mountain, and whistled a special whistle that was known by his friend, the eagle. The eagle lived in a nest high up in the mountain, and he flew down to Little Hiawatha's side. Little Hiawatha explained about wanting some feathers. The eagle was moulting—losing his warm-weather feathers, so as to grow thicker ones for the cold weather. In his nest were plenty of feathers that he had shed, so he brought some down to Little Hiawatha. The little Indian was delighted. He thanked the eagle, and hurried home to the Indian camp. There, one of the Indian braves showed him how to dip the tips of the feathers in red berry juice, to make them a pretty color. A squaw stitched them on to a headband for him. Little Hiawatha tried on his new headdress, and felt very grand indeed.

Little Hiawatha's daddy smiled when he saw him.

"You look very fine, my boy," he said. "One day, when you are grown-up, you will wear a headdress like mine every day, but for now you can wear your headdress on special days."

All the Indian braves came to look at Hiawatha, and to cheer him, and there wasn't a happier little Indian boy to be found in the whole land!

Scamp's New Coat

Scamp the puppy had a new, woolly, knitted coat. It was white and soft, and it kept young Scamp very warm and cozy. Scamp didn't really care for coats very much, but when the days began to turn colder he realized that he would appreciate it. One chilly autumn morning he set off to the park, wearing his woolly coat. Lady and the Tramp, his parents, went with him, and they felt proud of their smart little son. In the park, Lady, the Tramp and Scamp met Pongo and Perdita, the Dalmatians, who were out for a walk with their fifteen puppies. Pongo and Perdita stopped to talk to Lady and the Tramp, and the puppies stopped to talk to Scamp—at least, they stopped to *laugh* at him!

"You look funny in that knitted jacket, Scamp!" chuckled a puppy called Penny. The other puppies giggled and agreed.

"Do I really look funny?" asked poor Scamp.

He was so dismayed that he backed away from the Dalmatian puppies. He backed close to the park gate. But the gate was being painted just then.

"Watch out!" gasped the man who was painting.

The man was too late, for Scamp's beautiful white coat was spattered with large black spots of paint from the painter's brush. The painter was sorry, and so was Scamp. Scamp thought his warm coat was ruined, but a puppy called Freckles said:

"Now that you have black spots you look like a Dalmatian. You look like one of us."

"In that case," said Scamp, "I can't possibly look funny. All you Dalmatian pups look very grand indeed, and if I look like you, then I must be grand, too."

Scamp was soon strolling along behind the Dalmatian puppies, through the park, parading his new spots for everyone to see.

"I'm a spotty dog, too!" Scamp told Lady, the Tramp, Pongo and Perdita.

The Dalmatian puppies didn't laugh at him any more!

An Indian Summer

"**D**umbo," said Timothy Mouse, to his big friend, "will you fly me to the seaside, please?"

Dumbo, the flying elephant, looked surprised. He knows that Timothy Mouse is fond of the seaside, but he also knew that it was much too cold to go.

"The sea would be too chilly for paddling, Timothy," said Dumbo, "and it isn't the weather for sunbathing on the beach!"

Timothy, however, had made up his mind.

"Please, Dumbo, please, *please!*" he squeaked.

Now Dumbo is a kindly elephant, and he wanted to please Timothy.

"Very well, Timothy," he said. "Climb on to my back, and we'll be away."

Off flew Dumbo until, at last, they reached the seaside. They were tired when they arrived, and so they found a nice, cozy guesthouse where they could spend the night.

The next morning Dumbo was amazed to see that the sun was shining brightly. They hurried to the beach, and found that the sun was warm enough for sunbathing!

"We can even paddle in the sea!" said Dumbo, testing the water. "What a sudden change in the weather!"

"It is called an Indian summer," explained Timothy. "Sometimes, when everyone thinks summer is over, we have a surprisingly warm spell. An Indian summer was forecast on the radio, so I knew it was coming. That's why I wanted you to bring me to the seaside."

Now Dumbo understood, and what a grand time they had digging and paddling and lying in the sun! It was *wonderful*!

King Louie's Pumpkin Game

Is it true raisins are just worried grapes?

King Louie and his soccer team were ready to play soccer with their rivals—another team of monkeys.

Now, King Louie will do *anything* to make sure that his team wins. Before this particular match King Louie called his team together:

"Teeee! Heeeee!" he giggled. "I've painted this pumpkin with brown paint so that it looks just like a soccer ball. The other team will try to kick it towards our goal, when they see it, and meanwhile we will kick the real ball towards their goal, and score a goal. When the referee sees that they have only been playing with a pumpkin, he will say their goal doesn't count. Our goal will count, and so we shall be the winners!"

King Louie kicked the pumpkin soccer ball into play, and when the other team came along they did indeed think that it was a real soccer ball. The referee started the match.

One of the monkeys ran straight towards the pumpkin soccer ball.

King Louie and his team watched him eagerly.

THUD! The monkey's foot hit the pumpkin soccer ball. Then an unexpected thing happened! SQUELCH! His foot went right into the pumpkin, which was rather soft, and a huge spray of pumpkin flesh and juice went splattering all over King Louie and his team! Instead of hurrying with the real ball towards the other goal, King Louie and his wet monkeys were so taken aback by their surprise that they just stood still, and forgot about trying to score a goal. They were in such a mess, and they looked so funny, that the referee began to laugh. The other team began to laugh, too, when they realized what had happened.

But King Louie and his soggy monkeys didn't laugh. They were feeling much too wet and uncomfortable, and much too silly. They had to go home for a change of clothes and a bath. The game was canceled, so they didn't win, after all! It served them right, really, didn't it, for trying to cheat!

Those Cozy Afternoons!

Madame Bonfamille lives in a very grand house in Paris, and she has a lovely garden. In it is a beautiful summerhouse, where she sits on sunny afternoons. Her cat, Duchess, and Duchess's three kittens, Marie, Berlioz and Toulouse, all love the summerhouse! They like to lie on the warm, wooden floor and gaze out at the beautiful garden. The summerhouse is full of interesting things for the kittens to explore.

The kittens were sad, therefore, one autumn day, when Madame Bonfamille said:

"I think it's time for us to close up the summerhouse. We'll open it again next summer."

Madame Bonfamille asked her butler, Edgar, to take everything out of the summerhouse, sweep it clean, and lock the doors.

"Oh, I do feel unhappy now that summer has come to an end," sighed Marie.

Duchess, Berlioz and Toulouse felt sad, too. They followed Madame Bonfamille indoors, and she took them into her grand living room. Madame Bonfamille had asked Edgar to light a warm log fire in there, and the room felt very cozy. She placed a silk cushion in front of the fire for Duchess, and a soft rug where the kittens could sleep.

"Now," said Madame Bonfamille, "this is the time of year for tea beside the fire."

She asked Edgar to fetch tea.

"Ooh, there will be cheese for us, and cream, and perhaps even a ham sandwich each," Duchess told her kittens. "Autumn afternoons can be very cozy indeed, you know."

The kittens forgot about the summerhouse. They weren't sad any more, because they were busy looking forward to all the cozy autumn afternoons that lay ahead.

Lambert and His Frogs

Alice: "What starts with 'T', is full of 'T' and ends with 'T'?"
White Rabbit: "That's easy. A teapot."

Lambert the sheepish lion was sitting beside the pond, when suddenly he heard a plip! plop! plip! plop!

"Ooh," said Lambert. "Something splashed my nose."

"It was the frogs, my poppet," said Mother Sheep.

Mother Sheep has looked after Lambert since he was a baby.

"The frogs have jumped down into the bottom of the pond, where they will sleep until the warm spring weather comes again," Mother Sheep explained to Lambert.

To Mother Sheep's surprise, a large tear began to trickle down Lambert's furry nose. The tear plopped into the pond.

"Don't cry, my darling," said Mother Sheep. "What has upset you?"

"The frogs are my friends," said Lambert, who loves little creatures. "All summer I enjoyed watching them hopping about. Now I won't see them for months and months. Oh dear!"

"Then, Lambert my treasure," said Mother Sheep, "I shall tell you a story every evening—all about frogs. I'm clever at making up stories, you know, and I shall tell you stories about the Bad Frog, the Good Frog, the Sleepy Frog and the Happy Frog. I'll think of a story about a frog who wouldn't do as he was told, and I'll tell you one about a frog who loved to travel, and one who wouldn't learn to swim. You shall have a frog story on Mondays, Tuesdays, Wednesdays, Thursdays, Fridays, Saturdays and Sundays—all through the winter. Instead of having frog-watching time every evening, you shall have frog storytime, and you will enjoy it just as much, I'm sure. You won't have time to be sad about your little frog friends. Baaaaaa!"

Lambert stopped crying, and began to look forward to all the frog stories that Mother Sheep had promised to tell him.

"I think I am a very lucky fellow to have you for a mother," said Lambert to Mother Sheep. "I think you are the kindest sheep mother that ever a lion could have!"

Dumbo the Golfer

Dumbo is the little elephant who can fly, and he has a friend called Timothy Mouse. One day they decided to have a game of golf together. They had only just begun to make their way around the golf course when a squirrel came hopping slowly towards them.

"I've hurt my paw," he told Dumbo and Timothy. "Until it is better again I can't climb trees to collect my winter nuts. I know that you can fly, Dumbo, so please would you fly up to a tree and collect some nuts for me?"

Dumbo said that, of course, he would help the poor squirrel. He knew that all the squirrels would be going to sleep soon until the spring, and he knew that the little squirrel must have a store of nuts so that he could wake up now and then and have a feast.

Timothy and the squirrel watched as Dumbo flew to the top of a tall tree and hovered there, above the branches, flapping his ears just fast enough and hard enough to keep himself in the same place. Suddenly,

60

holding his golf club tight with his trunk, Dumbo swung the club back and back, and then swung it forward again very quickly so that it cracked down on a bunch of nuts, sending some of the nuts showering down to the ground. This Dumbo did again and again, until the ground beneath the tree was covered with nuts. Timothy and the grateful squirrel ran to the tree when Dumbo had finished, and Timothy helped the squirrel to gather them up and take them to his secret store in a hollow tree trunk.

Dumbo flew down and the squirrel thanked the little elephant for his kind help.

"That's quite all right," said Dumbo. "I enjoyed myself, and now I've had lots of practice with my golf club after all that nut hitting, I expect I'll hit the ball really well! Come on, Timothy—back to the golf course, to finish our game. Good-bye!"

Off went Dumbo and Timothy—and Dumbo played the best round of golf that he had ever played!

3
October

Apples with a Special 'Little Something'

In Christopher Robin's garden grew a large apple tree that was covered with ripe, juicy apples.

"We'll have stewed apples for our dessert today," said Nanny.

The next day they had stewed apples, and the next day, and the next. Christopher Robin and his Nanny thoroughly enjoyed them.

Now, each day Nanny prepared an extra bowl of apples for Christopher Robin to take to his friends, Winnie the Pooh, Eeyore, Piglet, Tigger and Rabbit, so that they could have some for their dessert. After a week of apples each day, Pooh complained:

"We've had apples for dessert on Monday, Tuesday, Wednesday, Thursday, Friday, Saturday, and now again today. Apples aren't exactly my favorite thing, you know."

"Nor mine," said Eeyore.

"Nor mine," said Piglet.

"Nor mine," said Tigger.

"Nor mine," said Rabbit.

Christopher Robin told Nanny, who said:

"Well, it's a shame to waste the apples. I'll make them different tomorrow. Each of your friends shall have a special 'little something' with their apples."

The next day, at lunchtime, Christopher Robin bought each of his friends a surprise. He gave Eeyore stewed apples with thistles, because he loves thistles. Pooh had apples and honey, because he loves honey. Piglet had apples and acorns, because he loves acorns. Rabbit had apples and grass, because he loves grass. Tigger had apples and extract of malt. Extract of malt is what Tiggers like best!

"Delicious!" they all said. "Thank you, Christopher Robin. We like apples, after all. May we have them again tomorrow?"

"Clever Nanny!" said Christopher Robin.

An Arrow in the Sky

Bambi, the baby deer, had wandered off into the forest. He loved looking at birds, insects, flowers and plants, and he had been watching them all so busily that morning that he had not noticed where he was going. Now he knew that he ought to be going back to his mother, but he wasn't sure which way to go! All the paths looked alike!

"I want my mother!" sighed poor Bambi.

Then he saw some swallows sitting on the branches of a tree.

"If they fly high up into the sky, they will be able to see which path I should take," thought Bambi.

As nicely as he could, Bambi asked the swallows to fly up and see if they could see his home in the distance. The swallows were eager to help, and up they flew, into the sky. As Bambi watched, he saw some of them fly one behind the other, to form a line. Then some of them made two little lines near the beginning of the first.

"Why, it's an arrow!" said Bambi. "The swallows have made an arrow to show me which way to go!"

Bambi followed the direction in which the arrow pointed until, at last, he reached his home, where his mother was waiting. They were thrilled to see each other, and the swallows were glad to have helped.

Now, if you should look up, one day, and see swallows flying in the sky, and making an arrow shape, some folks may tell you that that is the way swallows like to fly when they are about to go to a warmer country, but it may just be that they are showing some little lost animal the way home!

63

Daisy's Secret Present

Duchess: "A bar of soap please."
Goofy: "Certainly. Would you like it scented?"
Duchess: "No, I'll take it with me!"

Donald Duck was painting a sign in secret. No one knew what it said, but Huey, Louie and Dewey thought it might have something to do with Daisy's birthday.

And the day before Daisy's birthday, while she was out shopping, Donald got a man to fix something in her room. It was *another* big secret, like the sign he had painted.

On the day of Daisy's birthday party, Donald climbed on to Daisy's roof and fixed the sign up where everyone could see it. Then he went indoors and joined Huey, Louie, Dewey and Daisy for a birthday-cake snack.

"Happy birthday, dear," beamed Donald, pecking Daisy on the cheek. "Your present is already here."

"Thank you," smiled Daisy. "But WHERE is it? I can't see it."

"In a minute or two you should HEAR it," chuckled Donald.

64

"But what is it—and where have you hidden it?" chirruped the triplets.

"Be patient, boys, and you too, Daisy," grinned Donald.

Meanwhile, outside the house, Mickey Mouse, Goofy, Minnie, and all Daisy's Disneyland playmates had seen Donald's sign. It read: 'It's Daisy's birthday today. Her new phone number is Disneyland 321.'

Meanwhile, in Daisy's house she, along with Donald and the triplets, waited in puzzled silence. Then from a cupboard by the door there came a ringing sound.

Daisy waddled over to investigate, and when she opened the cupboard she was surprised to find a birthday-present telephone! Picking up the receiver, she answered, saying, "Daisy Duck here."

"Happy birthday, Daisy!" cried Mickey Mouse over the phone.

"Oh! What a lovely present!" gasped Daisy Duck, in between lots and lots of happy birthday phone calls!

IT'S DAISY'S BIRTHDAY TODAY. HER NEW PHONE NUMBER IS DISNEYLAND 321

65

No Jam for the Jam Tarts

The Queen of Hearts was *very* upset! She wanted to make jam tarts for tea, and she had the pastry ready, but she couldn't find any jam. She had searched every pantry in the palace, and all the cupboards, but there wasn't a jar of jam to be seen.

"You must have used it all, Your Majesty," suggested Alice.

"But how can I make jam tarts without JAM?" roared the Queen. "And I MUST have jam tarts!"

The Mad Hatter had a suggestion or two.

"How about filling your tarts with chocolate pudding instead? Or you could make porridge tarts!"

The Queen of Hearts said that the Mad Hatter must go away and stop being silly. She chased him through the palace and out into the garden. There, to make sure that he went away, she started tossing hard little apples at him. The Mad Hatter went, at last, and Alice picked up some of the apples.

"Why, these are crab apples," she said. "I remember my mother making crab-apple jelly with these. We used to eat it with bread and butter, like jam."

"JAM!" shrieked the Queen. "Then we'll make some straight away!"

The Queen set the Walrus and the Carpenter to work gathering crab apples, and made Alice go with her to the royal kitchens, where they began making crab-apple jelly. It wasn't very difficult, and the jelly was ready in time to make the tarts for a late supper.

"Crab-apple jelly tarts are simply lovely!" cheered the Queen.

Alice thought so, too, and so did the Walrus, the Carpenter and even the Mad Hatter, who had all been invited to share that very special meal.

Mickey and Minnie's Autumn Break

7 October

Mickey and Minnie Mouse had decided to have an autumn break—a little holiday—at the end of October.

"It will make us fit and well, and ready to face the winter," said Minnie.

"It will be cheaper than a holiday in the summer," said Mickey.

The two of them set off in Mickey's car to the seaside town where they were to stay. As soon as they arrived at their hotel they had to unpack their suitcases. They washed, and then changed their clothes, before hurrying to the dining room for their evening meal. There was a dance in the hotel that evening, and Mickey and Minnie danced every dance together. When bedtime came, they fell into their beds, very tired. The next morning Minnie wanted to look in the shops, and they bought presents to take home for Pluto, Goofy and Donald, and Daisy Duck. After lunch they decided to go for a drive in the car and look at the parts of the town they hadn't seen yet. It was a long drive, and they didn't arrive back at the hotel until it was time for their evening meal. That night they went to a theater to see a jolly seaside show. The next morning Mickey and Minnie hurried to the beach and went for a walk right along the sands. They arrived back at their hotel just before lunch, and afterwards they walked to the next town to look at the important and interesting buildings there. Then they ran back to their hotel for a meal, and a visit to another hotel for a musical evening. The next day there was more walking, shopping, driving and dancing, and on the day after that it was time for Mickey and Minnie to pack up their suitcases again.

"Mickey, I'm exhausted!" sighed Minnie. "We've done so *many* things in our few days here."

Mickey was worn out, too.

"Why did we come away for a rest?" he asked. "We would have rested more if we had stayed at home."

"Well, how about another autumn break," asked Minnie, "—to recover from this one?"

What a funny pair they are!

Clarabelle's Market Stall

Clarabelle Cow has a stall at the local market every Saturday morning. During the summer she had sold ice cream and milkshakes. You can imagine how glad the tired and thirsty shoppers were to be able to buy a cooling ice, or a glass of refreshing milk. Clarabelle enjoys running her stall, and she enjoys pleasing her customers. She usually looks forward to market day.

Minnie Mouse was surprised, therefore, when she called on her friend, Clarabelle, early one Saturday morning, and found Clarabelle looking miserable.

"Cheer up, Clarabelle!" said Minnie. "You'll be off to the market in a moment, and you always enjoy market days, don't you?"

"Not any more!" sighed Clarabelle. "You see, now that it isn't hot any longer, folks don't want to buy ice cream or milkshakes. They say that shopping makes them cold anyway, and they don't want to buy something that is going to make them even colder."

"Poor Clarabelle!" said Minnie. "But why don't you sell something HOT? You could still sell your milk if you heated it up, and put some chocolate syrup into it. I'm sure shoppers would love a mug of hot chocolate to warm them. Instead of selling ice cream, you could sell roasted chestnuts. There is a chestnut tree in our garden, and Mickey Mouse will make you a brazier—that's a special closed-in fire—for your roasting!"

Clarabelle thought Minnie's idea was simply splendid —and Minnie rushed home to pick sweet chestnuts, and to ask Mickey to set to work on the brazier.

By the next morning everything was ready. Minnie and Mickey were the first customers at Clarabelle's market stall.

"Hot chocolate for me, please, Clarabelle," said Mickey.

"A bag of roasted chestnuts for me, please, Clarabelle," said Minnie.

When the shoppers at the market saw those lovely warming things for sale, they hurried to Clarabelle's stall—and very soon Clarabelle Cow was just as busy and as happy as she used to be in the summertime!

Bambi's Antler Tree

Mickey: "Before getting off the bus what must you do?"
Morty: "Get on it!"

Bambi was now quite grown-up, and all the other animals called him the Prince of the Forest. Bambi always took an interest in his fellow creatures, and when he saw a great many birds flying through the forest to the birds' meeting place one morning, he knew that they must be gathering together before flying off for the winter. He knew that they would return to the forest again once spring had arrived, so he didn't feel too sad. Bambi watched as more and more birds gathered together. Soon every branch of every tree seemed to be covered with perching birds. There were large birds and small birds—hundreds and hundreds of them. The last to arrive at the birds' meeting place were several swallows, and they looked around for somewhere to perch.

"There isn't an empty branch anywhere!" gasped one of the swallows. "We could stay on the ground, but then we wouldn't be able to listen to all the other birds as they plan which way we shall fly. We want to be up high, near all the other birds."

Bambi, as Prince of the Forest, knew that he would have to help the worried birds somehow. Suddenly he held his head up high, and called to the swallows:

"Come! Come and perch on my antlers. There is plenty of room here for you, and you won't be too far away from all your friends."

The fine, strong antlers that had grown on top of the grown-up Bambi's head were shaped rather like the branches of a tree, and so the swallows perched there very happily indeed. They were able to listen to all the excited chatter of the other birds. Bambi listened, too, and was fascinated to know where the birds were planning to go, and how they were going to get there.

At last the birds were ready to set off on their flight. The swallows thanked Bambi for his help.

"You are good and kind, Bambi," they chirped. "No wonder all the forest creatures call you the Prince of the Forest!"

Goofy's Great Big Feet

Goofy never worries about being sloppy. He'll wander about in his oldest things, not caring who sees him, as long as he feels comfortable. One day, however, Mickey pointed out that he must have some new shoes before the winter weather arrived. His old ones were too scruffy to wear any longer. They had holes in the soles, holes in the toes, and the backs didn't fit around Goofy's heels at all.

Goofy hated shopping, and he sighed as he made his way to the shoe shop with Mickey.

"Well!" gasped the shop assistant, measuring Goofy's feet. "I only hope I can help you, sir. I'll bring you my biggest sizes."

The shop assistant looked among the largest boxes, and came back to Goofy carrying two.

"Try these shoes, sir," he said, opening the boxes. "This pair is large, and this pair is extra large."

Goofy put on the large pair, and walked about the shop.

"No," he said. "My toes feel crushed."

Then Goofy put on the extra large shoes.

"Ooo, ouch!" he grumbled. "They hurt me, too. What *am* I to do? I'll just have to go about barefoot! I wish I didn't have such great, big feet."

The shop assistant told Goofy that his new shoes would have to be a special size called largest-of-all. He would order them for him, he said, but it would take some weeks before they arrived at the shop for Goofy to pick up.

Mickey was worried about what Goofy would do in the meantime. Goofy could not wander around for several weeks in his present state. Mickey watched the shop assistant packing the largest shoes back into their boxes, and he noticed that the boxes were even larger than the shoes. Suddenly, Mickey took the shoes out of their boxes, and told Goofy to stand in the empty boxes. Mickey asked the shop assistant for some string, and with the boxes tied to his feet, Goofy could walk about happily.

"Now I have some shoes—sporty box shoes to last me until I get my largest-of-all pair," said Goofy. "Hurrah!"

Roo and the Apple Tree

Roo, the baby kangaroo, was feeling very pleased with himself. He had found an apple tree in the forest. It was the first thing Roo had ever found all by himself. When he saw the big, juicy apples he squeaked with delight.

"I'll come back tomorrow and bring my friends Winnie-the-Pooh and Piglet," Roo told himself. "They will know how we can pick the apples, and then we'll eat them all up."

Roo licked his little lips, and hurried back home to Kanga, his mother, because it was nearly his bedtime.

The very next day, as soon as he possibly could, Roo came hurrying back to the clearing in the forest where he had seen the apple tree yesterday.

But when he looked up at it he had a horrible surprise! There was not an apple on it—not one!

"Someone has picked them all!" wailed Roo, "and that someone wasn't me!"

Winnie-the-Pooh and Piglet came wandering through the forest just then, and they found poor Roo sobbing. Roo told them about the missing apples.

Pooh and Piglet couldn't seem to comfort poor Roo, and so they decided to take him back to Kanga.

As soon as Pooh and Piglet and Roo walked into Kanga's kitchen they smelled a delicious smell.

"Mmmmmmmmmm!" sniffed Pooh. "Apple pie!"

"Quite right!" smiled Kanga. "I went for a little walk when Roo had gone to sleep last evening, and I found an apple tree. I picked the apples, and now I'm making an apple pie for Roo's lunch. Would you like to stay and share it with us, Pooh and Piglet?"

Of course, Pooh and Piglet said they would, and Roo said he wanted a big slice of apple pie that very moment. It was a gorgeous pie, and they all thoroughly enjoyed it.

"If Mummy hadn't picked the apples instead of me," said Roo to Pooh and Piglet, later, "we wouldn't have had that lovely pie. So I'm very glad she did pick them."

Pooh and Piglet rubbed their tummies and were very glad too!

Cinderella's Huge Task

Cinderella's Ugly Sisters had yet another job for her to do!

"Pick all the apples from the orchard!" they told her. "Polish every apple, and put them away in the attic, on trays, to store for the winter."

The Ugly Sisters didn't offer to help Cinderella.

Poor Cinderella set to work. It was hard having to pick all those apples and by the time Cinderella had filled three large baskets she was very tired.

"I don't think I have enough energy left to polish all these apples and put them on trays and carry them to the attic," Cinderella told her Ugly Sisters.

"You must!" they shouted. "We are going out, and we shall leave you here to finish the work."

They left Cinderella alone in the kitchen with the three baskets of apples—but she wasn't alone for long! Suddenly, Cinderella's Fairy Godmother appeared!

"Don't worry, my dear," said her Fairy Godmother. "I am here to help. Bring me twelve birds from the garden."

Beagle Boy: "I'm free, I'm free!"
Michael: "That's nothing, I'm four!"

74

Cinderella was puzzled, but she did as she was told. The birds are her friends, so she opened her window and called twelve of them into the kitchen. Her Fairy Godmother waved her magic wand, saying:

"Bibbadi, bobbadi, boo!"

Instantly, the birds became dear little page boys!

"Now do Cinderella's work for her!" said her Fairy Godmother.

Each page boy picked up a cloth and polished an apple, and put his polished apple on a tray. The page boys went on doing this until all the baskets were empty and the trays were full. Then they each carried a tray up to the attic, where the apples were to be stored for the winter.

When the page boys returned, Cinderella's Fairy Godmother turned them back into birds, and they flew into the garden.

"Oh, Fairy Godmother, good-bye and thank you!" said Cinderella.

When Cinderella's Ugly Sisters returned they were surprised to see that all the work was finished.

"That's fast work, even for Cinderella!" they said.

They didn't guess what had really happened. Only Cinderella, her Fairy Godmother, the birds, and YOU know that!

The March Hare's Dance

The merry March Hare had decided to hold a dance for all his Wonderland friends.

"It will be a Grand Ball," decided the March Hare. "It will be held at the Queen of Hearts' palace, in her ballroom. I will rent a dinner suit for the occasion."

The merry March Hare hurried to the Wonderland Rental Shop, and asked for a dinner suit, his size. The shop-bunny looked him up and down.

"Now, let me see! You will need a tall, thin suit," he said.

He pulled a suit from his cupboard, and told the March Hare to try it for size. The March Hare put on the suit, and he *did* feel uncomfortable! He wasn't used to wearing a suit, you see, and this very stiff, extra-fancy one just didn't feel right. The collar felt so hard that he could hardly turn his head, and his ribs felt all shut in so that he could hardly breathe. He tried sitting down and even that was difficult. Walking about in those neat trousers felt strange, too.

Bambi: "How can you tell a poisonous snake from a harmless one?"
Thumper: "By the bite!"

"If I can't walk or sit—how ever am I going to dance?" sighed the March Hare. "I do so enjoy leaping and jumping and twisting and twirling and dancing."

The March Hare tried on several suits, but he didn't like any of them.

"I'd much rather wear my usual rough-and-tumble clothes!" he said.

"Then how about having a Tramps' Supper instead of a Dance," suggested the elegant shop-bunny rather rudely, "or a Barn Dance."

"That's it! A Barn Dance!" cheered the March Hare.

"Everyone can come in jeans and T-shirts. Everyone will be comfortable. A Barn Dance will be just right for this time of year, because we can make cider, and serve potatoes-in-their-jackets, and apple pies."

The March Hare took off the dinner suit, and hurried on his way around Wonderland, to tell everyone about the Barn Dance.

"We'll hold it in the royal barn, instead of the ballroom," he said.

Everyone thought that the Barn Dance was a splendid idea—and everyone had a wonderful time, including the merry March Hare, of course!

A Bargain that Wasn't a Bargain

Clarabelle Cow: "Do people fall off here often?" **Guide:** "No madam, only once!"

M r. Toad was picking up his car from the local garage, where it had been for repair. (Toad's car is always having to be repaired because he *will* drive it far too fast.) He was just about to leap into his car and drive away, when he noticed that the shop opposite had a GRAND SALE. Now, Toad is never one to miss a bargain, so he left his car where it was, and crossed the road to the shop. He discovered that the shopkeeper was selling off his leftover summer clothes, ready to make way for the new winter lines. There were lightweight suits at half the original price, as well as half-price swimming trunks, sun hats, shortsleeved shirts and sandals.

"These things are too good to be missed," Toad told the shopkeeper. "I'll have two lightweight suits, three pairs of swimming trunks, two sun hats and three pairs of sandals."

Toad paid for his bargains, and staggered out of the shop with them. He piled them into his car, and sped off for Toad Hall. His friends, Ratty and Mole, were waiting there for him, and he showed them his bargains.

"But Toad, old chap, what is the use of these summer

clothes now that autumn is here?" asked Mole. "It's far
too cold to wear them."

"You could put them away and save them for next
summer," suggested Ratty.

Toad, however, is not a fellow to put things away. He
wanted to wear his new clothes at once. He tossed them
back into the car and leaped in after them.

"Then I'm off," he called, "off to a warm South Seas
island where I can wear my bargains. I'll drive to the
airport, and catch a plane that will take me to the other
side of the world where it is summer now."

"But Toad, dear fellow, if you've got to spend a lot of
money on an expensive holiday simply so that you can
wear your bargains—then they're not bargains, after all.
They'll cost you more than if you had paid full price for
them at the proper time of year," said Mole.

"What? Can't hear a word you say, old chap!" called
Toad, who had started his car engine once more. "Good-
bye now—I'll see you both in a few months!"

Away he sped, into the distance! What a funny Toad
he is!

Potatoes-in-their-Jackets

Huey: "Which side of a cake is the left side?"
Louie: "The side that hasn't been eaten!"

Wart was a boy who lived long ago, in the days when brave knights walked the land. Wart was the adopted son of a kindly knight named Sir Ector, and Wart had a half brother named Kay.

Wart was much younger than Kay, and very young boys sometimes make mistakes. The mistake that made Kay laugh most of all happened when Sir Ector said to Wart:

"I think we shall have potatoes-in-their-jackets for supper, Wart. Will you fetch some, and take them to the cook?"

Wart liked to please Sir Ector, and he hurried away at once. He had never heard of potato-jackets, but he went first to ask the gardener.

"No, I only have shirts and breeches!" laughed the gardener.

Puzzled, Wart went to the cook and asked:

"Where do I buy potato-jackets, please?"

"From a potato-jacket shop, I should think!" chuckled the cook.

Wart wondered at their merriment. Then he saw Kay in the distance and ran to him.

"Where do I find the potato-jacket shop?" asked Wart.

"There's no such place!" giggled Kay. "When Father said he wanted potatoes-in-their-jackets, he meant he wanted the potatoes cooked in their skins. The whole potato is popped into an oven to cook. Even I know that! In summertime we have new potatoes that are small, and have to be peeled, but now that the year is nearing its end the potatoes are large—big enough to be cooked in their jackets!"

Now Wart understood! He hurried back to the gardener and asked for some large potatoes. He took them to the cook, who popped them into her hot oven and left them there for an hour or two. When suppertime came the cook took them carefully from her oven and brought them to the table, wrapped in cloths.

Sir Ector sliced open the potatoes. He put butter and cheese on top of the fluffy, white potato, and it melted there. When the potatoes-in-their-jackets were cool enough to eat, Sir Ector, Kay and Wart had the most delicious potato feast!

"I think that potatoes-in-their-jackets are the nicest potatoes of all!" beamed young Wart.

No More Baseball!

Goofy was feeling very sad indeed. The baseball season had ended, you see, and Goofy had washed his baseball suit, and put it away for the winter. Goofy wasn't a very *good* player, but he *did* enjoy playing!

"Now I'll have nothing to do all winter!" he grumbled, one morning.

Mickey felt sorry for his big friend.

"I wish I could think of something that would cheer him up again," said Mickey to himself. "Now, what is there that could take the place of baseball for Goofy? What about soccer, I wonder? If I could get a team together, then perhaps we could interest Goofy in soccer. It is the soccer season now, after all."

By the time the afternoon came, Mickey had gathered together his friends, Pluto and Donald Duck, and Donald's three nephews, Huey, Dewey and Louie, as well as Minnie Mouse and Mickey's own nephews, Ferdie and Morty.

"Now, when Goofy joins in, we can have a five-a-side soccer match," said Mickey.

Practical Pig: "The Big Bad Wolf was pushed down a well yesterday!"
Fifer Pig; "Are the police looking into it?"

At first Goofy thought that soccer wouldn't be much fun after baseball, but when he had played for a time, he began to think he might enjoy it, and by the end of the match he was a keen soccer fan!

"I'll knit soccer sweaters, shorts and socks in team colors for us all," promised Minnie. "Let's play every week."

Goofy agreed!

"Now I shall enjoy the soccer season just as much as the baseball season!" cheered Goofy.

Too Much Television!

On sunny, summer afternoons Pongo and Perdita's fifteen Dalmatian puppies had been happy to play together in the garden. Now that the days had grown shorter and cooler, however, they only wanted to stay indoors and watch television.

"Our puppies would watch television all day and all night, too, if I let them," Perdita told Pongo.

Pongo smiled, and told Perdita that she worried too much. He followed Perdita into the living room, where all fifteen puppies were watching a program about a superdog.

Suddenly, Roger and Anita, their owners, came into the room and switched off the television.

"We've something to tell you all," said Roger. "You have been asked to make an advertisement for television, for a new brand of dog biscuits."

Roger, Anita and Nan brushed Pongo and Perdita and the puppies, and then a truck arrived from the television

84

company to take them all to the studio.

The camera crew worked away, and Roger and Anita had to look at the cameras and say that they thought the biscuits were good for dogs and puppies. Then the cameras were directed at Pongo and Perdita and their puppies, who had to eat a bowl of the biscuits between them, and then smile and wag their tails to show that they had enjoyed them. Everything went well, and afterwards all the Dalmatians went happily home with Roger and Anita, who had been given enough dog biscuits to last their pets for a whole year!

When the advertisement was shown on television for the first time, Pongo, Perdita and the puppies were *thrilled* to see themselves on the screen.

"Didn't we do well!" chuckled a puppy called Freckles. "It was because we had watched so much television that we knew just how to behave in front of the cameras."

All the other Dalmatians just had to agree!

Lampwick Learns a Lesson

L ampwick was a naughty lad, looking for something naughty to do, when he saw some acorns growing on a huge, old oak tree.

"I'd like some of those," thought Lampwick.

Now, instead of coming back in a day or two when the acorns were ready to fall, and instead of waiting until he could pick up the acorns from the ground, Lampwick decided that he must have them *at once*! He looked around for the biggest stones and sticks that he could find, and he began hurling them up into the tree. He knocked down several acorns, and also three branches which had been broken off by Lampwick's sticks and stones.

Little Jiminy Cricket, Pinocchio's friend, came along just then.

"Ooh, Lampwick," said Jiminy. "Spoiling trees is a bad thing to do."

"Poof! It's only an old oak!" sniffed Lampwick, not caring.

"But, Lampwick, that giant oak has taken hundreds of years to grow to that size," explained Jiminy. "Now you come along with your sticks and stones and in just a few moments you do all that damage."

When Lampwick realized how long the tree had taken to grow, even *he* felt sorry that he had tried to spoil it.

"How can I make up to the old oak for what I have done?" asked Lampwick.

"Well, you could help some more oak trees to grow," said Jiminy. "If you plant some of those acorns, then in hundreds of years there will be more old oaks in this spot for folks of the future to enjoy."

Lampwick poked his finger into the leaf mould on the ground, and he popped an acorn into the hole he had made. He did this several times.

"Now, when you're a grown man, Lampwick, you can come back here, and you will see that your acorns have grown into oak trees. They won't be giant oaks by then, but they will be taller than you will be. They will be company for the old giant."

Lampwick did return to that place when he was a grown man, and he saw that Jiminy's words had come true. Several sturdy little oaks were growing beside the giant oak. The giant was now very old indeed, and as Lampwick looked up at it he felt sure the giant waved its branches to him in a friendly way!

87

Dumbo to the Rescue

Little Timothy Mouse and his big friend, Dumbo the flying elephant, were out together one day, when Timothy said:

"Let's fly high in the sky!"

Dumbo just flapped his big ears, and off he flew, with Timothy on his back. Over houses they went, over streams and over fields. In one field, Timothy noticed a big combine harvester.

"That means the corn is ready to be harvested," said Timothy.

Suddenly, Timothy remembered that he had some fieldmouse cousins living in that field.

"Dumbo, we must get the fieldmice out of the field before the great, noisy combine harvester frightens them!" cried Timothy.

At once, Dumbo flew down to the edge of the field. The driver of the combine harvester was talking to the farmer, before he started work.

Now, Timothy knows how to whistle loudly. He put two claws in his mouth, and blew very hard down the gap between them. All the fieldmice in the field heard that whistle and knew it meant danger. As quickly as they could, they made their way through the barn to Timothy's side.

Timothy explained about the combine harvester, and told the fieldmice to climb on his friend's back. Then the kind elephant flapped his big ears, and flew them all away to another field where there was no corn.

"Thank you so much, Timothy and Dumbo," said the mice. "Tomorrow, we'll make ourselves new homes. But now we are tired. It's getting late and we must sleep."

They lay down in two lines on the grass, and Dumbo spread out his soft ears over them, to make cozy blankets to keep them warm. Timothy crawled under an ear himself.

"*Dear* Dumbo," yawned Timothy, "good-night."

Tinkerbell the Teacher

The Queen of all the fairies sent for Peter Pan's little friend Tinker Bell, one day.

"In my palace there are two baby fairies who are ready to learn to fly," said the Fairy Queen. "Please teach them for me, Tinker Bell."

Of course, every fairy has to do what the Fairy Queen tells them to do.

Tinker Bell thought her job would be an easy one. She held one baby fairy in each arm and flew with them to a tree. She put them on a branch, and stood beside them.

"Flap your wings, and off you go!" said Tinker Bell.

The baby fairies just looked at Tinker Bell, and they would not move!

"Oh dear!" thought Tinker Bell. "They're frightened. What shall I do?"

Now, the leaves were beginning to fall from the tree and as two leaves floated down past Tinker Bell, the fairy had an idea.

She picked two of the nearest leaves and she sat a baby fairy on each leaf. She gave the leaves a gentle push, and the leaves floated down towards the ground.

"*Wheeeeeeeeeeeeee!*" chuckled the babies. "What a lovely ride. Floating down through the air is very nice."

When the babies reached the ground, Tinker Bell flew down to them.

"Yes," she smiled, "it is nice to float through the air. Now let's see if you can do it without the leaves."

Tinker Bell took the babies to a high branch once more. Then she said:

"Off you go!"

This time, they *did* jump!

"Flap your wings!" called Tinker Bell.

The baby fairies did flap their wings, and how they enjoyed themselves!

"We're flying! We're flying!" they called. "Thank you, Tinker Bell! Thank you!"

The Leaf Collectors

Bernard and Bianca, the mice, were having a holiday in the home of a kind lady. They had once led an exciting life, working for the International Rescue Aid Society, and now they were happy to lead a quiet life.

Their hostess's pride and joy was the pond in the middle of her lawn. Bernard and Bianca were distressed, one day, when they saw her staring at her pond in a worried way.

"Just look at all those leaves!" she said, to herself. "The pond is almost covered with dead leaves. They look untidy!"

She removed the leaves from the edge of the pond, but she couldn't reach the middle ones. Bernard and Bianca were fond of her because she had helped them in the past and she always made sure that there were crumbs left near their mousehole.

"We must help her, dear," said Bianca to Bernard. "Let's fetch Evinrude."

Evinrude is a dragonfly, and he was spending the holiday with Bernard and Bianca.

"Evinrude," said Bianca, "if Bernard and I climb into that large leaf that is turned up at the edges, would you propel us across the pond, my sweet?"

Evinrude watched as Bianca and Bernard climbed into their leaf-boat, and tied another large leaf onto the back of it. Evinrude grabbed hold of the stem of the leaf at the back, and propelled both leaves across the pond.

"Now, go slowly, Evinrude, my love!" said Bianca. "Then Bernard and I will have time to pick up the dead leaves. Bernard, dear, put them into the leaf-boat we are towing!"

Bernard, Bianca and Evinrude worked very hard until the pond was clear of leaves. Bernard and Bianca removed their leaf-boats from the pond, and the mice and the dragonfly all collapsed, very tired, on the bank of the pond. Evinrude puffed and panted for fifteen minutes until, at last, he got his breath back!

The kindly lady was delighted when she saw that her pond looked tidy again.

"Perhaps the wind blew the leaves away," she said.

But *we* know who it was really, don't we!

The Stormy Night

Eyore had his own little house. Christopher Robin had built it for him. It was made of branches.

"It's quite cozy really," Eeyore told everyone; "at least, as cozy as a rather drafty house in the middle of such a gloomy field can ever be."

Although Eeyore didn't sound very thrilled with his little home, he was very sad indeed when, one very stormy night, the wind blew it down! Fortunately, Eeyore wasn't hurt, but his little house was ruined! The branches were bent and broken, and Christopher Robin said he didn't think he could rebuild it.

"That sort of thing always happens to me," grumbled Eeyore. "Someone gives me something reasonably nice, and then it is taken away from me again."

"Now, Eeyore!" said Christopher Robin. "Don't be so sorry for yourself. We'll soon find you a new home."

Christopher Robin asked everyone in the forest if they had any ideas for a new home for Eeyore. Winnie the

Pooh couldn't think of anything—neither could Kanga
or Roo. Tigger and Rabbit couldn't help either, but Owl
knew the very thing!

"A large tree was blown down in the storm last night,"
said Owl. "I know because I happened to be perching
near it at the time. It was a hollow tree, and would make
a splendid house for Eeyore."

Christopher Robin thanked Owl, and took Eeyore to
the place where the tree had been blown down. The
trunk was huge and, at the bottom, completely hollow.
Eeyore climbed inside the hollow part. It was roomy and
dry, and it made a good shelter from the wind and rain.

"Not bad!" said Eeyore. "I suppose it would do as a
place for someone who doesn't mind living in the old,
broken-down remains of a tree."

Christopher Robin smiled. Eeyore always pretends to
be sad and gloomy, but Christopher Robin guessed that
he was secretly delighted with his new home.

Christopher Robin, of course, was quite right!

Thumper, the Nutcracker

Bambi's rabbit friend, Thumper, is called Thumper because he is very good at stamping one foot up and down very fast on the ground, and it makes a sort of thumping noise. Thumper does this when he wants to call his friend, Bambi, to him, or when he wants to warn any of the other animals that something is happening.

One day, Thumper used his thumping foot in a rather unusual way. It all began when a squirrel came to Thumper. The squirrel, you may remember from another story, had hurt his foot. He wouldn't even have been able to gather any nuts from the trees if it hadn't been for the help of Dumbo, the flying elephant, who flew up to the tree for him. Well, thanks to Dumbo, the little squirrel had plenty of nuts for his winter store, and he had gone to sleep happily. Halfway through the autumn, he had awakened, and decided to have something to eat, but because his paw still wasn't quite healed the poor little chap was unable to crack any of his nuts.

Napoleon: "Why is Captain O'Hara up the tree?"
Scat Cat: "He's been transferred to a Special Branch!"

"I want a little feast before I go back to sleep for the rest of the winter," he sighed. "What am I to do?"

"Don't worry," said Thumper. "I can crack your nuts for you."

"But I've never heard of a rabbit cracking nuts!" gasped the squirrel.

"Maybe not, but my thumping foot is very strong, after all that thumping I have done, and I can do unusual things with it," said Thumper.

So saying, he began thumping his thumping foot up and down on top of the squirrel's nuts.

Crick! Crack! Crick! Crack! The shells split under the weight of Thumper's thumping foot.

"Now I can have my nut feast! Now I can have my nut feast!" squealed the squirrel with joy.

He was soon munching away very happily and Thumper went off to find his friend, Bambi.

"I am the best nutcracker in the whole forest!" said Thumper, very proudly indeed.

The Runaways

Paul Bunyan: "Do I need training to be a litter collector?"
Goofy: "Nope! You just pick it up as you go along."

On a farm in the country lived Sergeant Tibbs, the cat, and his friends, Captain, the horse, and Colonel, the dog. Their master, the farmer, is kind, and for *years* he has fed them at midday, every day. Sergeant Tibbs has milk and cat-food, the Captain has water, hay and oats, and the Colonel has water and dog-food. Although the three of them couldn't tell the time, each of them knew when it was midday. Their tummies suddenly felt hungry and empty, and they would go to the farmhouse gate to meet their master with their food.

One day, however, they knew it was midday, but no master appeared. They waited and waited, growing more and more hungry.

"Where is our food?" grumbled the Captain.

"Our master must have forgotten us," sighed Sergeant Tibbs. "He just doesn't care about us any more, and is never going to feed us again."

"Then we must go away and find someone who will feed us and look after us," said the Colonel.

"Quite right!" said the Captain. "Come along, you chaps."

96

Sergeant Tibbs, the Colonel and the Captain began hurrying down the hill away from the farm when, suddenly, they heard a voice calling them.

"Hey, come back, you three. Where are you off to? Don't you want your meals?"

There was the farmer at the gate, with his animals' meals on his truck.

Sergeant Tibbs, the Colonel and the Captain came back at once, and as they watched him putting their food and drinks into their bowls and buckets he said:

"Did you think I had forgotten you? No, the clocks have been changed, you see. We were on daylight saving time, but now we are on standard time, which means that today's meal has really come an hour later—although it is still midday by our clocks. So it's twelve o'clock, not one o'clock, as you must have thought."

In their animal ways, Sergeant Tibbs, the Colonel and the Captain understood, and they knew that everything was all right again. Their master still loved them and was going to care for them always—and not forget their meals.

That day, the three funny friends enjoyed their midday meal even more than usual!

Changing the Clocks

In the spring we put our clocks forward one hour, to give the farmers extra daylight in the evening, so that they can get all their work done. In autumn we put the clocks back again.

This year, when it was time to put the clocks back, every clock had been changed—EXCEPT ONE! This was the tall town clock in the town where Pluto, Goofy, Mickey Mouse and Donald Duck were spending their autumn vacation. The mayor of the town was worried, for there wasn't a ladder there that was long enough to reach the top of the clock tower.

"We could send for the fire company from the next town," said the mayor. "They have very long ladders, but that would be expensive."

"Don't worry," said Mickey. "We'll make an animal ladder to reach the hands of the clock."

"An animal ladder?" said the Mayor.

"Yes," said Mickey. "I'll show you how it's done."

Mickey told Goofy to stand up straight, at the bottom of the clock tower. Then Mickey told Pluto to climb on to big Goofy's strong shoulders. Next, Mickey climbed on to Goofy's back. After that, Donald climbed on to Mickey's shoulders.

"You see," puffed Donald, from the top, "an animal ladder!"

Donald was level with the face of the clock and was able to turn the hands back one hour, so that the clock showed the same time as all the others.

"Hurrah!" cheered the mayor. "Well done, all of you!"

Down climbed Donald, Mickey, and Pluto, very pleased with the job they had done.

98

An Enormous Puddle

It had been raining heavily, and in the courtyard of Prince Charming's palace there was a huge puddle that stretched right across the width of the courtyard. Cinderella and her handsome Prince husband didn't realize the puddle was there—otherwise they would have gone to the rescue of their little friends Gus and Jaq, the mice. You see, Gus and Jaq had been out for the night, and now they wanted to return to Prince Charming's palace, where they lived, but they couldn't cross the courtyard because of the puddle. It was much too deep for them to wade across, there was no way around it, and mice don't like swimming!

"What shall we do?" wailed Gus. "I'm hungry and I want to go home."

Jaq looked around for something to help them. There was a buckeye tree nearby, and a buckeye had fallen to the ground below it. The green shell had split in half, showing the brown, shiny seed inside. Jaq hurried over to it. He didn't want the seed—just the green, prickly outer shell.

"You carry one half of the shell to the puddle, Gus, and I'll carry the other," said Jaq. "Be careful, they are very prickly."

Very carefully indeed, the two mice took the shell to the puddle. There, Jaq climbed into his half, and sat in the soft, white inside. Then Gus climbed into the other. He had quite a struggle to get into his half, because he is plump. At last he managed, and Jaq said,

"Now, paddle with your paws, Gus. We'll soon be across the puddle."

The two mice splashed away with their paws, and the two halves of the shell, like two tiny rowboats, floated over the puddle, and were soon safely on the other side.

Gus and Jaq jumped out of the shells, and cheered:

"Now we can go home, to Cinderella, Prince Charming *and* our breakfast!"

99

Mickey's Leaf Mountain

Edgar: "The invisible man's outside."
Duchess: "Tell him I can't see him."

Mickey Mouse was once an apprentice to a Sorcerer—a magician who could do all sorts of magic.
One day the Sorcerer asked Mickey to sweep up the leaves that were lying in his garden. Mickey began sweeping, but he grew tired, and decided to try to make the broom do the sweeping by itself! Remembering some of the magic that the Sorcerer had taught him, Mickey uttered a spell:

"Broom, Broom, in just a while,
Sweep all these leaves into a pile!"

At once the broom began sweeping, and soon there was quite a pile of leaves in a corner of the garden. The pile of leaves was soon HUGE, and there were no more leaves scattered over the lawn.

"I must stop the broom now," said Mickey, "but I can't think of a suitable spell!"

The broom kept on sweeping, and it brought the leaves

from the garden path *and* the pavement outside the garden to the pile. The pile of leaves grew higher!

"It's a leaf mountain!" gasped Mickey.

Then, luckily for Mickey, the Sorcerer returned, and he said a spell to make the broom stop sweeping:

"Broom, Broom, stop working NOW!
Please stand still, and take a bow."

The broom did as it was told, and there was no more sweeping done.

"Now, what shall we do with all those leaves?" said the Sorcerer. "I think we'll *leave* them where they are! They will be useful to you, one day, Mickey."

Mickey grew puzzled, as days , weeks and even months went by. In fact, a whole year passed by before the Sorcerer said:

"Now we can make use of the leaf mountain, Mickey."

By now the leaves were soft, dark and moist. The Sorcerer told him to dig the leaves into his flower beds, because the leaf mould would make the earth good and rich, so that bulbs and flowers would grow nicely.

Mickey dug the whole of the leaf mountain into the garden soil, and the following spring he had the most wonderful display of flowers!

Mickey was glad his leaf mountain had been useful, but he made up his mind never to meddle with magic spells again!

Nuts for the Pudding

The Mad Hatter was having yet another of his many tea parties. This time he had invited the Queen of Hearts, and Alice and the Dormouse, as well as the March Hare, of course, who went to all his tea parties.

Alice arrived before the Queen of Hearts, and she found the poor Mad Hatter in a very worried state.

"What's the matter?" she asked him.

"I have forgotten to buy some nuts for the pudding!" sighed the Mad Hatter. "I know that the Queen of Hearts likes to have lots of raisins in her pudding, and nuts on the top, sprinkled over the whipped cream. I remembered to buy everything—but not the nuts. The Queen of Hearts will be here at any moment! Oh dear me!"

"Well, there should be plenty of nuts about at this time of year," said Alice, at once.

Alice looked around her, and, sure enough, she soon saw a tree that was laden with hazel nuts. She looked on the ground under the tree, but no nuts had fallen there.

"I wonder how we can reach some?" said Alice.

"The Dormouse could reach them. He can climb trees," suggested the Mad Hatter. "Let's wake him."

Alice thought this was just another of the Mad Hatter's crazy ideas, but to her surprise, when the Mad Hatter had lifted the Dormouse out of the empty teapot where he slept, and awakened him, the Dormouse began to climb the tree! He worked away with his sharp little teeth and his claws, and sent a shower of hazel nuts down to the ground. Alice picked them up, shelled them, washed them, and popped them on the top of the Mad Hatter's pudding. She managed to do all this just before the Queen of Hearts arrived. The Queen was very glad to see the nuts on the pudding, and she and everyone else enjoyed the tea party—except the Dormouse, who, having eaten several hazel nuts, had gone back to sleep!

"Well!" thought Alice to herself. "Fancy a dormouse climbing a tree! I learn something new every day in Wonderland!"

The Useful Acorns

Two little pigs, called Fifer and Fiddler, were rolling about happily in the fallen leaves. But the third pig, called Practical Pig, was busy collecting the acorns that had fallen from an oak tree. Soon Practical Pig had lots of acorns, and he spread them out on the grass, so that the sun could dry them.

"You *are* busy!" said Fifer. "What a lot of hard work! Whatever do you want all those acorns for?"

"It's my winter supply," explained Practical Pig. "I'm going to store them away, and when there is snow on the ground, and there isn't much for us pigs to eat, I shall take my acorns out of their store, and eat them. You and Fiddler ought to do the same."

Fifer said: "It sounds too much like hard work. We won't bother to do that."

Fifer and Fiddler are *not* practical pigs! They went back to their leaf rolling, and Practical Pig went back to his acorn collecting. None of them saw the Big Bad Wolf coming across the grass towards them.

"Ah!" thought the Big Bad Wolf. "*Now* is my chance to catch those three little pigs!"

The Big Bad Wolf didn't see the acorns on the ground, and he stepped right on some of them. His feet slid away from under him, and he fell with a BUMP! He was quite a time picking himself up and rubbing his bruises, and while he was doing that the three little pigs, who had

heard the bump, had time to run to the safety of Practical Pig's brick house.

"Hurrah!" puffed Fifer, when they were indoors. "What a good thing you collected those acorns, Practical Pig. If you hadn't been so practical in preparing for the winter, we might have been caught by the Big Bad Wolf. Some of your acorns are crushed, but you still have plenty left for the winter. Will there be enough for you to share some with us when winter comes?"

"Of course," said Practical Pig, who is kind.

It's a very good thing that Fifer and Fiddler have Practical Pig to look after them, isn't it?

105

Edgar's Wicked Trick

Edgar is Madame Bonfamille's butler, and he is *not* good! He is always trying to steal away her cat and kittens, because he wants her to leave her money to him rather than to her cats. Madame Bonfamille adores Duchess, the cat, and Duchess's three kittens, and so it was bad of Edgar to plan his wicked plan. He decided to dress up as a wicked Halloween wizard to frighten Madame Bonfamille!

"She'll be so scared that she'll do anything I say," Edgar chuckled. "I'll demand that she give me her pets. Then I'll take them away and lose them!"

By the time Halloween was near Edgar had made himself a cloak and pointed hat, with star patterns on them, a mask, and a pretend magic wand. In his room Edgar dressed himself up and crept downstairs. Madame Bonfamille was in the sitting room with her precious pets, and Edgar planned to leap in there.

Before he reached the bottom of the stairs, however, the door opened suddenly, and out came what Edgar thought was a *witch*! He did not know that it was really Madame Bonfamille dressed up! She was going to a Halloween party, you see, and she had just been showing her outfit to her cats.

"Oh dear!" shrieked Edgar. "A witch!"

He sped to the bottom of the stairs, down the hall, through the kitchen, and out of the back door, and wasn't seen again for days! As for Madame Bonfamille, she had realized the figure on the stairs was Edgar the moment he had shrieked.

"He must have been going to a Halloween party, too," she thought. "I didn't mean to scare him!"

She didn't guess that her butler had really been trying to frighten her!

The Party Lantern

Maid Marian and Robin Hood had been making a pumpkin lantern for Halloween. They planned to have a party and invite their Sherwood Forest friends to it, and the pumpkin lantern was to light the table. They hollowed out the pumpkin, and cut eye shapes and a nose and mouth. They stood the lantern where their guests would see it when they arrived. Carefully, they put a lighted candle inside it.

"It looks splendid!" said Robin.

He and Marian busied themselves with the party preparations. Neither of them knew that, at that moment, their three enemies, the Sheriff of Nottingham, Prince John and Sir Hiss, the snake, were creeping through the forest towards them.

"This-s-s-s-s-s time we'll capture Robin and Marian," hissed bad Sir Hiss. "They won't s-s-s-s-s-s-see us creeping up on them now that it is nearly dark."

Suddenly, all three of them stopped, and remained very still, staring into the distance.

"W-w-w-w-w-w-what's that I see?" stammered Prince John, in a worried way. "It l-l-l-l-l-l-looks to me like something frightening."

"Let's-s-s-s-s-s not wait about here any longer. I don't like the look of that fierce face," hissed Hiss.

The Sheriff agreed, and the three of them sped away through the forest. What they didn't realize was that the frightening face they had seen was only the pretend lantern face, and could not harm them at all. It was Robin and Marian's pumpkin lantern that had sent their three enemies away! Robin and Marian, not knowing about the danger they had been in, just enjoyed their party as if nothing had happened. All their guests admired the pumpkin lantern, but none of them realized just how useful it had been!

A Halloween Procession

The Reluctant Dragon is a friendly fellow who doesn't want to fight, or frighten people. He just likes to keep quietly to himself, reading his poetry.

The villagers in his neighborhood told him, one morning, that they wanted his help.

"All of us have been invited to a party given by the mayor of a nearby town," said one of the villagers. "We thought it would be nice to have a special Halloween Procession. We could all march to the mayor's parlour, wearing our witches' hats and our pumpkin masks. We thought that perhaps you would lead the Halloween Procession and breathe flames of fire, as dragons do, to light our way for us."

The Reluctant Dragon scratched his head.

"Er—I would like to help you, you understand—but, you see, I don't actually breathe flames of fire—not actually. I know most dragons do, but I'm a reluctant, gentle dragon, and I don't have such powers. My fire

108

went out a long time ago, through lack of use, and I don't think I could get it started again."

The villagers were so disappointed that the Reluctant Dragon tried to think of a way to help them.

"In my garden," said the Reluctant Dragon, "are some special plants called Chinese Lanterns. I grow them because dragons come from China, and we like Chinese things. If you each pick one of these little lantern shaped flowers, and ask a lightning bug to sit inside it, you will each have a bright lantern to light your way for the Halloween Procession."

The villagers said that they would do as the dragon suggested, and they were so grateful for his idea that they asked him to come with them to the party, and share the party fun.

"I'll come with you," said the Reluctant Dragon, "just as long as everyone promises not to frighten me with a pumpkin mask!"

What a gentle, timid, unusual dragon he is!

The Yum-Yum Crusher

Wendy, John, Michael and the Lost Boys were all playing happily by the Never-Never Land river, when suddenly all of them were frightened by a large, green crocodile which came gliding through the shallow water towards them.

They all went scampering away to find Peter Pan, to complain to him about the crocodile.

"I'll see that he doesn't harm any of you!" said Peter, at once. "He must be the crocodile who swallowed a clock—the one who likes to chase Captain Hook."

Peter hurried to the river, to find the crocodile. There, Peter stretched out his arms and sang a song:

"As sure as Peter Pan's my name,
Smile, crocodile, for now you're TAME!"

At once, the crocodile was all smiles.

"I'm so sorry I frightened Wendy, John, Michael and the Lost Boys," said the crocodile. "If you forgive me, I will do something nice for you. *Tick-tock!*"

"We do forgive you," said Peter. "And I know what you can do for us. Over there is a yum-yum tree. It is covered with large fruits called yum-yums. They ripen in the

autumn, and crushed yum-yums make a delicious yum-yum drink. If Wendy and I pick the yum-yums from the tree, will you crush them for us with your strong tail?"

The crocodile said he would be glad to help. As soon as Wendy and Peter had picked all the yum-yums and put them in a tub, the crocodile came out of the mud and swung his heavy tail as high as he could, and then whacked it down on to the huge fruits. He did this again and again, until the tub was filled with empty yum-yum skins, and lots of yum-yum juice. Peter removed the skins, and then he cut reeds from the river bank and made them into drinking straws. He gave one each to Wendy, John, Michael and the Lost Boys. He had one, too, and so did the crocodile. They all put their straws into the tub, and drank and drank. The yum-yum juice was *delicious*!

When every drop of yum-yum juice was gone, the crocodile crept away into the river again.

"You've given me such a lovely drink that now you're all my friends!" smiled the crocodile. "I'll never ever frighten any of you again. *Tick-tock!*"

111

Alice: "But what does the orange do when it stops rolling?"
The Queen of Hearts: "Looks round, of course!"

Silver and Gold

Uncle Scrooge had bought himself a telescope. Night after night he would gaze through it at the stars, and people were beginning to talk. Was Uncle Scrooge taking an interest in something OTHER than money?

Donald Duck went to see him. When he opened the door Uncle Scrooge looked starstruck! "You're watching those stars much too much!" warned Donald.

"Bah! I suppose you're right!" admitted the old duck, dizzily. "But what if I am?" he snapped. "Whose business is it, anyway?"

"No one's," Donald reassured him. "But aren't you going to invite me in?"

"Very well," muttered the old duck. And so they went inside. The place was in a TERRIBLE mess.

"Uncle Scrooge," said Donald sympathetically, "you

look as if you've had no sleep for a week. What on earth have you been doing?"

"I found a message on my doormat," muttered the miser. "It told me that the stars were made out of the purest silver."

"Whoever heard of such a thing!" chuckled Donald. "Let me see this note."

So the old skinflint showed Donald the grubby note.

"This is Beagle Boy handwriting!" declared Donald. "While you've been staring through your telescope they've probably . . ."

Uncle Scrooge ran like greased lightning into his gold room. "Help! Police! Robbery!" came startled quacks.

"What's happened?" cried Donald.

"They've stolen a whole chest of gold," muttered Uncle Scrooge angrily, "while I was watching the stars!"

"Never mind, Uncle," chuckled Donald, who knew that Scrooge had more money than he'd ever need. "There's a lesson here. If you hadn't been so greedy that you wanted to steal the silver from the stars, your *own* gold would still be here!"

Work for Orville

Orville the Albatross was feeling bored. He didn't have anything to do, you see.

All the birds who like to go abroad for the winter had gone. He had helped one of them, but now there was no more work of that sort to be done. No one else wanted to travel abroad in the winter, so there was no reason for him to fly to another country.

"I do enjoy flying!" sighed Orville. "I know it's a bit of an effort for a large bird like me to get up into the sky, but once I am there, I really love it."

Orville told everyone he met how miserable he felt, and the news of Orville's lack of work spread far and wide.

A robin came to hear of Orville's trouble, and he went to him with an idea.

"All my bird friends have gone abroad for the winter," said the robin. "Mrs. Robin and I would like to get in touch with them. We'd like to send them a letter to say that we are well, and we'd like them to send letters to us

FLY ALBATROSS AIR LINES

to say how they are getting along. Would you fly to and fro with letters, Orville?"

"You mean be a sort of air mail carrier?" said Orville. "Ooh, I'd like that very much. It would mean plenty of work all winter through. Just bring me the letters, Mr. Robin, and I'll be off."

The robin returned that very afternoon with letters from himself, his wife and all his robin relations. They were all to be taken to friends overseas.

Orville had a little carrier strapped to his back, into which the robin popped all the letters. Then he watched as Orville tried and tried and tried to get himself up into the air. At last, Orville was away, soaring between the clouds.

The robin didn't see Orville again for a week, but then he returned with letters for the robins from all their friends overseas.

"Isn't this exciting!" said Orville. "Oh, I do so enjoy being Orville the airmail carrier!"

Big Bloomer

Goofy slumped in an armchair, frowning fiercely. "Huhh!" he sighed.

"What's the matter, Goofy?" asked Mickey Mouse, anxiously. "Have you got a pain?"

"No!" grunted Goofy. "I'm thinking, and thinking is hard work!"

"Can I help?" asked Mickey.

"I'm thinking what to give Minnie for Christmas!" Goofy muttered, scratching his head.

Mickey was astonished. "But it's only NOVEMBER!"

"Yes," Goofy agreed. "But last year I forgot all about presents until Christmas Eve, and there was nothing left in the shops. This time, I've thought of something for everyone—except Minnie!"

"Minnie loves flowers," smiled Mickey. "Plant some bulbs in a bowl now, put them in a dark, airy place, and they will bloom for Christmas!"

That afternoon, Mickey called again. On Goofy's kitchen table lay four, small, empty boxes. Mickey looked at them in surprise! "Oh no!" he groaned. "I don't believe it!"

Mickey hurried into the garden shed, where Goofy was placing a bowl on the lowest shelf. "I've planted the bulbs! Pretty pink ones!" burbled Goofy excitedly. Mickey peeped at the tips of the bulbs, just showing above the soil.

"Er—yes! That's fine, Goofy!" he gulped. "Just fine!"

That night, Mickey crept into Goofy's shed with a bowl just like the one Goofy had used for his bulbs. Mickey picked up Goofy's bowl, and put his own in its place on the shelf. Then he tiptoed away.

Safely back at home, Mickey pushed aside the dirt in Goofy's bowl and took out—*four pink electric light bulbs*!

"I might have known Goofy would get it wrong!" chuckled Mickey. "But I didn't have the heart to tell him about his big 'bloomer'!"

So kind Mickey had replaced Goofy's bowl with another, in which nestled four pink hyacinth bulbs. "Goofy won't be disappointed now," Mickey smiled, "and Minnie will be delighted with her present!"

A Laugh for Eeyore

Eyore's gloomy place looked even more boggy and sad now that the cold, dull days had come to the Forest. Eeyore stood with his donkey tail between his legs, and his ears down.

Winnie the Pooh looked at him and sighed.

"Oh, Eeyore, cheer up!" pleaded Pooh Bear.

"Why?" sniffed Eeyore.

"Because . . ." said Pooh.

That didn't help the miserable donkey at all, so Pooh had to think of something else.

"I'll make up a cheering-up song for him," decided Pooh.

Pooh thought for a moment, and then began to sing:
"DON'T BE SAD,
'CAUSE IT'S VERY BAD
TO BE SO SAD.
YOU OUGHT TO BE
A HAPPY LAD.
BE FULL OF JOY—
A CHEERFUL BOY
THEN I'LL BE GLAD
THAT YOU'RE NOT SAD."

"Is that it?" asked Eeyore. "Is that to cheer me up?"

"It is!" beamed Pooh. "I'm rather good at songs, and I think that is one of my best. It might even be one of the best songs in the whole world!"

"The best song in the whole world!" snorted Eeyore. "Well, I think it's the *worst*! It's the worst song I've ever heard! It's laughable that you should think it a good song, really laughable!"

In fact, Eeyore thought it so laughable that he began to laugh in a hee-haw donkey kind of way. He was laughing unkindly and he was laughing at Pooh, but Pooh did not care. At least Eeyore was laughing—that was the main thing. Eeyore hadn't laughed for ages.

"You can laugh at me as much as you like, Eeyore, as long as you laugh!" said Pooh. "I'd rather hear a laughing donkey than a moaning donkey!"

Pooh hurried away to tell Christopher Robin that he had actually made Eeyore laugh. Christopher Robin agreed that he must be a very clever bear indeed!

Maid Marian's Trail

The bad Sheriff of Nottingham and his friends, Prince John, and the snake, Sir Hiss, had captured Maid Marian!

"We'll take her to the castle, and keep her prisoner," said the Sheriff.

Marian was worried as she was led away. A rope had been tied around her waist, and the end of the rope was fastened to the back of Prince John's carriage. As this strange procession made its way through the forest, Marian tried to think of a way of telling Robin where she was being taken.

She looked about her, and was immediately attracted by the dark red elderberries that were growing on either side of the lane along which they were traveling. Marian grabbed handfuls of the little berries and began dropping them behind her as she walked. Prince John, the Sheriff and Sir Hiss, sitting inside their carriage, did not

know what was happening. They were not to know that Marian was trying to make Robin follow her. Her trail led to the Prince's castle, where Marian was taken to the dungeon. She did not have to stay there long, luckily, for when Robin was searching the forest for her he saw the strange little trail, and realized that it was some sort of message. He jumped onto his horse and followed the trail to the castle. It was nighttime when Robin arrived, and his enemies were asleep. A few tired soldiers had been left to guard Marian. Robin left his horse, swam across the moat, climbed up a castle wall and in through a tiny window. As he searched the castle, he heard Marian crying in the dungeon. Robin took the soldiers by surprise. They were so surprised that their cries for help came too late. Robin and Marian were away before the soldiers could summon help. Robin helped Marian out of the window, down the wall and across the moat. They leaped onto Robin's horse, and away they sped back to the camp.

"Hurray for elderberries!" cheered Robin. "We must celebrate!"

Friar Tuck fetched a bottle of his special homemade wine from the store—it was elderberry wine, of course!

119

The Firewood Adventure

Wicked Cruella de Vil had captured lots of Dalmatian puppies yet again! Once before she had captured them and they had escaped, but now they were firmly under lock and key in her crumbling country mansion. Cruella loved fur coats, and thought Dalmatian fur would make lovely ones! She had driven to London to see a coat maker, and left Horace and Jasper in charge.

"We must escape before she comes back!" said a puppy called Rolly.

Suddenly, Horace and Jasper unlocked the huge front door, and told the puppies to follow them outside.

"Don't try to escape," said Jasper, "or we'll chase you in our car and bring you back. We're taking you outside because we need help carrying firewood to light a warm, cozy fire indoors. We can't carry it all from the woods to the house. Our car can't manage the hill, but you dogs can each carry some firewood."

Horace and Jasper led the puppies to the woods, and gathered pieces of firewood to give to each puppy. The puppies staggered uphill with their burdens. Then Lucky, the smallest puppy, could carry his log no longer.

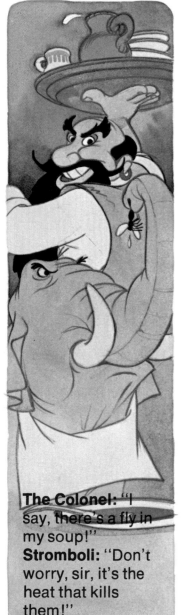

The Colonel: "I say, there's a fly in my soup!"
Stromboli: "Don't worry, sir, it's the heat that kills them!"

He let it fall, and it rolled downhill until it reached the
feet of Jasper, who had just begun to climb the hill.
Jasper tripped over the log and fell down.

Rolly had an idea.

"All of you!" he told the other puppies. "Drop your
firewood—NOW!"

Each puppy did as it was told, and the hill was covered
with rolling logs and branches. Horace was knocked
down, and so was Jasper. They couldn't stand up among
all that rolling wood.

"*Run!*" barked Rolly.

The puppies ran through the woods, across a ditch,
over a stream and into a field. When Horace and Jasper
got to their feet, the pups were out of sight, and the men
didn't know *where* to start looking.

The puppies ran until they met Pongo and Perdita, the
grown-up Dalmatians, who were looking for their fifteen
puppies.

"We're so glad you are safe," said Perdita. "Now we'll
take you all home."

As Pongo led the way Rolly told him all about the
exciting firewood adventure.

Swapping Sweaters

Bambi: "Why does a rabbit have a shiny nose?"
Thumper: "Because its powder puff is at the other end."

Minnie Mouse had knitted a sweater for Mickey. "You'll need something warm to wear now that summer is over," she told him. "Will you try it on, please? I want to see if it fits you."

Mickey was pleased with the bright red sweater, but when he put it on it was MUCH too big for him! It looked more like a large dress on him than a sweater! Poor Minnie *was* disappointed.

"I thought it would be the right size for you, but it's *enormous!*" she sobbed.

"Don't be sad, Minnie," said Mickey. "We'll take it to Donald Duck. Perhaps it will fit him."

Mickey and Minnie took the large red sweater to Donald, who tried it on, too, but it was much too big. Donald suggested taking the sweater to Pluto—so he, Minnie and Mickey set off to find Pluto. Pluto tried on the sweater, but it was even too big for him!

"Let's take it to Goofy," said Pluto. "Perhaps it will fit him."

They all went to Goofy, who put the sweater on, and it fit perfectly!

"I'm pleased about that," said Goofy. "You see, I needed a new sweater for the autumn. I have just washed the sweater I wore last autumn, and it shrank in the wash. Now it's far too small for me. Perhaps it would fit one of you."

Pluto tried on Goofy's small blue sweater, but it was too short for him. Donald tried it, but it was too short for him. Mickey put it on, and it was just the right size!

"Now Goofy has a new red sweater, and Mickey has a new blue sweater!" chuckled Minnie. "Things usually work out well in the end, don't they!"

Money Isn't Everything

Donald, Daisy, Huey, Louie and Dewey all went to visit Uncle Scrooge one cold autumn day. They knocked at the door and had to wait a long time before all the bolts were undone. Even then Scrooge looked very suspicious, as if they were Beagle Boys in disguise. The old miser was very surprised to see them all.

"Well, well. I suppose you'd better come in." he croaked at the door.

"Have you got a sore throat, Great-Uncle Scrooge?" chirped Louie.

"Don't be cheeky, Louie!" scolded Daisy.

"Stuff and nonsense!" croaked Uncle Scrooge. "I *have* got a sore throat! The young lad's right."

"Sorry to hear that, Uncle," said Donald sympathetically. "Should I send Dewey out to get you some cough drops?"

Kaa: "What do cannibals play at parties?"
Shere Khan: "Swallow my leader!"

124

"No. They cost too much money nowadays," complained the old miser. "I'd rather suffer the tickle in my throat."

"You don't seem very happy, Uncle Scrooge," soothed Daisy.

"Mind your own business!" snapped Scrooge.

"Poor old Great-Uncle Scrooge," chirped Dewey, who had jumped up to sit on his Great-Uncle's knee.

"What do you mean—*poor* Great-Uncle Scrooge!" chuckled Scrooge. "I've got more money than Fort Knox."

"What I meant," explained Dewey, "was that I had a sore throat too, and I hardly have ANY money. But I bought some cough drops." With that Dewey pulled out his box of cough drops and gave them to Uncle Scrooge.

"You can have my cough drops, Uncle," smiled Dewey, "because they cured *my* sore throat."

Uncle Scrooge didn't know *what* to say. But one great big tear rolled down his face.

"Poor Great-Uncle Scrooge," echoed the triplets.

125

Two Funny Scarecrows

Tweedledum and Tweedledee had been wandering through the countryside, enjoying the fresh air and admiring the views. Just as they were passing a large field Tweedledum said:

"Look! A scarecrow!"

The scarecrow was a pretend man, made by the farmer to frighten birds away and stop them from eating the winter wheat he had just planted.

"Those ragged clothes look fun! Let's try them on," said Tweedledee.

Tweedledee took off his cap and put on the scarecrow's old top hat. It was squashed out of shape and had several holes. The scarecrow wore an old shirt that had lost its collar and cuffs. Tweedledee put this on, as well as the knitted sweater that had started coming unknitted. Tweedledum tried to put on the scarecrow's shabby trousers, but he could only manage to get them half on, because Tweedledum has a very large middle! He also held the scarecrow's patched umbrella. The scarecrow's arms, legs and body had been made of sticks, tied together. Tweedledum untied the string, and began pretending to have a doublehanded sword fight with

Chief O'Hara: "What are your parents' names?" **Wart:** "Mummy and Daddy."

126

them. Then the funny fellows took the turnip that had once been the scarecrow's head, and tossed it back and forth to each other. When the farmer came by his field he was very upset to see that his scarecrow had been taken apart.

"You bad boys!" he told Tweedledum and Tweedledee. "If the crows have nothing to scare them away they'll eat all my winter wheat."

Tweedledum and Tweedledee were very sorry. They hadn't meant to be naughty, but they hadn't stopped to think.

"We'll be your scarecrows instead," said Tweedledum and Tweedledee. "We've spoiled yours, so that's the least we can do." They stood, on each side of the field, with their arms outstretched, and in the shabby clothes they looked like a pair of fat scarecrows! The farmer thought they looked very funny, but they certainly did a good job keeping the winter wheat safe, for when the crows saw the Tweedledum and Tweedledee scarecrows they began to laugh in a *caw-caw* sort of way. They laughed so much that they forgot about trying to eat the winter wheat! The farmer *was* pleased!

Donald Duck's Bonfire

Donald Duck had been clearing his garden and was busy building a bonfire from all the rubbish when his three nephews, Huey, Dewey and Louie, arrived. Straight away, those naughty little nephews began racing around the pile of leaves, twigs and garden rubbish and every now and then they stopped to pull some bits and pieces off it!

"I invited you to come and see the bonfire tonight, but you're being so mischievous that it wouldn't be safe to let you near it when it's lit," said Donald.

Huey, Dewey and Louie thought that they would have to stay indoors all evening and miss the fun. They were very surprised, however, when, just as it was growing dark outside, Donald came to fetch them and said, "Put on your warmest, oldest clothes, and follow me."

The three nephews did as they were told and soon they were following their uncle out of the house, across the garden and into the greenhouse.

"But, Uncle, we want to watch the bonfire!" moaned Huey.

The ducklings were even more surprised when Donald went out of the greenhouse, locking the door behind him!

"Why has Uncle locked us in here?" wailed Dewey.

Suddenly, Louie said: "LOOK! Uncle's setting light to his bonfire. See—over there! Now it's burning beautifully, and we can watch it very well from here. Uncle must have put us in here because he thought it would be too chilly for us outside."

Huey, Dewey and Louie never guessed that their uncle had really locked them in the greenhouse to keep them out of mischief, and to keep them safely away from the bonfire!

"Now I don't have to worry about my naughty nephews, and I can enjoy the bonfire, too!" chuckled Donald, happily.

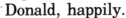

The Pumpkin Holiday-Home

Cinderella's handsome husband, Prince Charming, had bought a beautiful old-fashioned caravan from some gypsies. The gypsies had a new, modern one, but Cinderella liked the old caravan. It was gaily painted, with huge wooden wheels, and a little ladder leading up to the front door.

"Do let's go for a holiday in it, straight away. It would be nice to have a break before the winter," said Cinderella.

She and Prince Charming packed their holiday things into the caravan, and off they set, on a caravan tour. They had said good-bye to Gus and Jaq, Cinderella's little mouse friends, who lived at the Prince's palace with Cinderella.

"I don't like traveling," said Gus, "but I would like to spend the night out of doors in a special holiday home."

"I don't think mouse-size caravans are made," sighed Jaq.

Then Jaq remembered seeing something in the kitchen garden that would make a splendid holiday home for the two mice. Jaq took Gus to the vegetable garden, straight away.

"Look, Gus," he said, "a pumpkin! Help me roll it to that grassy place beside the pond and the rock garden. We'll eat out the juicy pumpkin flesh, and then the empty skin will make a little house."

The two mice were soon enjoying a pumpkin feast. They made 'windows' in the shell, and a 'doorway'.

"It looks just like a house—our very own holiday house!" cheered Gus.

He and Jaq had a lovely camping holiday beside the pond, and they explored the rock garden every day.

"I like your pumpkin caravan!" said Cinderella, when she and Prince Charming had returned from their caravan holiday.

"And so do we!" squeaked Gus and Jaq.

Mr. Toad's Wallpaper

Mr. Toad set out one morning to choose some wallpaper for his bedroom. In a local store he found a design that pleased him very much. It was an autumn leaf design, and the leaves were such lovely colors—red, yellow, gold, and brown.

"That leafy wallpaper would look good in my bedroom," Toad thought.

He bought ten rolls—enough for his bedroom—and returned at once to Toad Hall. Now, Toad isn't a fellow to do things himself when he can pay someone else to do them for him. He had a team of wallpaperers standing by, and they set to work at once on the bedroom. When they had finished, Toad thought it looked very grand. In fact he liked those colorful leaves so much that he asked them to decorate all the other bedrooms with the same paper. The store's delivery van brought lots more rolls of leafy wallpaper to Toad Hall. At last the bedrooms were ready!

"The trouble is," said Toad, "that the bedrooms are so

bright and cheery they make the bathrooms look dull."

Toad insisted that the bathrooms, too, be decorated in the same way. Then he said:

"Well, we might as well have the landing, stairs and hall all done to match."

The wallpaperers worked busily to carry out Toad's instructions.

"I suppose he will want the living room done next," sighed one of the wallpaperers, "and the dining room, study and library."

The wallpaperer was right! Soon there were more leaves inside Toad Hall than there were outside!

Toad's grand home has two kitchens and a laundry room—and, of course, Toad decided that they would all look nice papered in leafy paper.

When, finally, every room in the house had leafy walls, Toad still wasn't happy—and wanted some hung in the garden! The wallpaperers had had enough by this time, so they took their wages and went. Toad was left on his own—and how he enjoyed himself winding leafy wallpaper around the trunks of the trees! He laid strips of it along the paths, and even papered the garden walls!

Ratty and Mole thought it looked like the strangest garden ever!

"Toad really loves his leafy wallpaper, doesn't he?" laughed Ratty.

A Shivering Scarecrow

Chip 'n' Dale, the two little chipmunks, were walking across a field together one autumn afternoon when they saw a scarecrow with a very sad expression on his face. As they came closer they saw that he was shivering!

"I'm c-c-c-c-c-cold!" sighed the scarecrow.

He began to tell Chip 'n' Dale his unhappy story:

"In the spring the birds took my straw for their nests. I was once stuffed with straw, you see. In the warm summer I didn't miss the straw, but now that the cold season is here again I miss it ever so much."

"Poor Scarecrow!" said Chip. "We shall have to find something to stuff your old jacket and trousers with —you can't stand here in the middle of this bleak field with nothing to protect you from the wind."

Chip 'n' Dale looked around them, and Dale said:

"Look! There's a haystack in the next field. Let's take

some hay from it. Hay will be useful to our scarecrow friend and I'm sure the farmer won't mind if we take some. After all, the scarecrow does a good job for him, guarding his crops."

Chip 'n' Dale hurried over to the haystack, helped themselves to a pile of hay and hurried back to the scarecrow with it. They stuffed some into his jacket, and some into his trousers. They even lined his old hat, and they poked hay into the holes in his boots.

When Chip 'n' Dale had finished, the scarecrow looked very much more plump, and a great deal warmer. His clothes had been too thin and worn to keep him cozy, but now, at last, he was comfortable.

"Thank you so much, Chip 'n' Dale," said the scarecrow. "The hay will keep out the winter drafts."

The scarecrow had stopped shivering, and now he was smiling—very happily indeed!

The Singing Island!

Donald Duck was very fed up. He had had one cold in the head after another, ever since autumn had come. The damp, chilly weather seemed to bring on his wheezes and sneezes, and poor Donald didn't like having coughs and colds.

"I wish I could go away to a sunny island," he said to himself. "I would like to have a *warm* winter!"

Donald decided to ask another duck, called Moby Duck, to take him to sea in his boat.

"We'll find a sunny island and stay there together for the winter," said Donald—which made Moby very happy.

Now, Moby Duck's boat was a funny, tumbledown boat. He and Donald packed into it some things that they would need on their island, and off they set, across the ocean.

After a time, Donald pointed to a dark shape on the horizon.

"I think I can see an island!" cheered Donald.

Clarabelle Cow:
"People who throw kisses are lazy."

At last they reached it, moored Moby's boat and climbed onto what they thought was the island. Donald and Moby were just telling each other what a splendid place they had discovered, and how they would spend the winter there in the sun, when suddenly the island seemed to raise itself out of the water, and began to SING!

"There's no place like home!" sang the 'island'! "There's no place like home!"

Suddenly, Moby Duck and Donald realized that they had not landed on an island at all, but on Willie, the famous singing whale!

The whale's sweet song about home had made both the ducks feel homesick.

"Let's go home, Moby," said Donald.

Moby Duck agreed.

"Home may be rather cold at the moment," said Moby. "But, after all, it *is* home, and, as the song says, there's nowhere like it."

They said 'good-bye' and 'thank you' to the whale, slid down his back, climbed aboard their boat and set off for the shore again, just as fast as they could go!

Lambert's Woolly Lined Cave

Lambert is a shy and sheepish lion. He had been brought up from babyhood not by lions but by sheep. Because he had lived with sheep for so long, Lambert was not a bit fierce, and all the sheep loved him—which was why they wanted to help him when they found him shivering in his cave one autumn morning.

"The f-f-f-f-f-f-floor of this c-c-c-c-c-c-cave is c-c-c-c-c-c-cold!" stammered Lambert. "It's because it is made of s-s-s-s-s-s-stone, I s-s-s-s-s-s-s-s-suppose!"

"Don't worry, Lambert, my pet," said one of his sheep friends at once. "We sheep will see that you are soon warm again. Baaaaaaaaa!"

The sheep whispered a plan to her friends, and then all the sheep climbed down the rocks from Lambert's cave and back into their field. Then they began hurrying around the field, each sheep taking a piece of wool from the wire fence. You see, sheep's wool often catches on a wire fence as they pass, and little tufts get left behind. It was these tufts that the sheep took to Lambert.

"Line the floor of your cave with this wool," the sheep told Lambert. "Then your cave home will be cozy and snug. Baaaaaaaaaaaaaa!"

Lambert always does as his friend tells him, and the floor of his cave was soon covered with the little tufts of white wool.

"Anyone would think that it had been snowing in here!" chuckled Lambert. "It does feel cozy and warm and soft. I wouldn't be a bit surprised if I'm not the only lion in the whole world to have a woolly lined cave!"

The Nighttime Job

Princess Aurora had been asleep for a hundred years. She had been put to sleep by a trick played by the wicked fairy Maleficent. Handsome Prince Philip had finally awakened her with a kiss. Now Princess Aurora had married him, and they were very happy, except for one thing—Princess Aurora didn't want to sleep any more!

"No one would—not after a hundred years!" said Princess Aurora. "I've had enough sleep to last me for ages!"

Prince Philip, however, did need his sleep, and he couldn't sleep with Princess Aurora pacing around the bedroom. She tried going out for walks, but it was cold out at night. After two months of reading two books a night, she grew tired of that too.

When autumn came, Prince Philip had an idea. He sent his two servants to fetch all the acorns they could find. At last one of the palace rooms was filled with acorns.

"Now, dear," said Prince Philip to Princess Aurora, "how about spending some of your sleepless nights polishing those acorns, making holes in them and threading them on strings to make necklaces for us to sell to the ladies of our kingdom—then we should have enough money to pay some gardeners to clear our garden of hedges and weeds."

Princess Aurora thought this was a good idea. The garden hadn't been attended to for a hundred years, and it would take a great many gardeners to turn it back into a garden. Princess Aurora set to work that night. The ladies of her kingdom liked the acorn necklaces, and Princess Aurora sold so many that she and Prince Philip were able to hire a team of gardeners. Princess Aurora spent the autumn nights making acorn necklaces, and the gardeners spent the autumn days working in the garden. By the time the spring came it looked very nice, and Princess Aurora and Prince Philip spent each day in the garden. All that fresh air cured Princess Aurora of her sleeplessness, and now she sleeps so well at night that, once again, they call her the Sleeping Beauty!

Dopey's Fairies

Dopey, one of the Seven Dwarfs, was sitting on the grass under a tree. He had been watching the birds flying south to a warm country for the winter. Now he was tired of watching the birds, and he decided to find something else to watch. Suddenly, a little wing-shaped thing came floating by his face.

"Why, it's a fairy!" said Dopey, excitedly. "I must go straight away and tell Snow White that I've seen a fairy!"

Dopey hurried away to find Snow White, and she came at once to see what had excited Dopey so much. Then she, too, saw a little wing-shaped thing flying through the air.

"Oh, Dopey, you are funny! That's a sycamore seed, falling to the ground from the tree above. Did you see one, and think it was a fairy?"

Dopey had to agree that he had made a mistake. The other six dwarfs, who had come along with Snow White to see the 'fairies', all began to laugh at Dopey.

But Snow White said Dopey had given her an idea.

"We'll go on a seed hunt!" she said. "We'll see what other interesting seeds we can find."

Apart from the little winged sycamore seed, Snow White and the Seven Dwarfs found acorns, which are seeds from oak trees, seeds from horse-chestnut trees, fluffy dandelion seeds, a pine cone full of pine tree seeds, and rose hips, which are seeds from wild roses.

Snow White and the Seven Dwarfs found their seed hunt very interesting indeed, and they were all glad that Dopey had made his funny mistake!

189

The Thanksgiving Pudding Wish

Happy: "Penny for your thoughts?"
Doc: "No, I don't want to turn pro."

Winnie-the-Pooh called to see his friend, Kanga.

"Hello, Pooh dear," said Kanga. "I'm just making a Thanksgiving pudding for Roo and me to eat when Thanksgiving comes. When it's mixed I'm going to boil it, cool it, and then store it away. You may give it a stir. As you stir, make a wish and your wish will probably come true. Thanksgiving pudding wishes often do."

Pooh took Kanga's wooden spoon and gave the mixture a big stir.

"I wish," said he, "for a big jar of honey—extra specially nice honey!"

Pooh stopped stirring, and opened his eyes.

"Well?" he asked. "Where is my honey?"

"It may not come straight away, Pooh dear," said Kanga. "Wishes aren't always granted at once."

Pooh went away, feeling first disappointed, but then hopeful. Kanga went back to her Thanksgiving pudding stirring, and Roo began to eat his watercress sandwiches.

It was a day or so later, when Kanga had forgotten all about Pooh's wish, that Christopher Robin brought a large parcel to Kanga's home.

"The postman left it at my house for you," Christopher Robin told Kanga. "It's come all the way from Australia."

Kanga could hardly wait to open the parcel. Inside, she found a note from her cousin, who had sent a food parcel of lovely Australian foods. There was some butter, cheese, a can of peaches, a can of pears and a jar of honey.

Kanga wanted the butter and cheese, and Roo said he liked peaches. They gave the pears to Christopher Robin.

"Pooh would like the honey!" squeaked little Roo.

Kanga, Roo and Christopher Robin all arrived at Pooh's house, just a while later, as Pooh was searching his pantry and wondering what to have for breakfast.

When Pooh saw the honey jar he gasped:

"My wish has come true!"

Pooh tasted his Australian honey, and it really was delicious—*and* extra special. Pooh was so pleased that he made up a little song about it:

"I stirred a pudding and wished for a treat.
I wished for this honey, so sticky and sweet.
So now I'll stop singing, and just EAT and EAT!"

A Home That Couldn't Be Seen

Bambi had many friends in his forest home, and one of them was a wise owl. By the time Bambi was grown up and had become the Prince of the Forest, Owl had grown very old and a little short-sighted. It was then that a very strange thing happened. It all began when Owl decided to do some traveling.

"I must fly to the surrounding forests to visit all my owl relations, just once more before I am much too old," Owl decided one spring.

Owl was away from Bambi's forest for the rest of that year, and most of the next year, too. It was autumn of the following year by the time Owl, at last, returned to Bambi's forest. Owl had lived for many years in the top of an old, ruined tower. It was quieter than living in a tree, because the other birds didn't bother him there, and Owl had a splendid view of the forest from his tower. Now, however, all that Owl could see was a lot of greenery!

"There seems to be a tree in place of my tower!" Owl told Bambi sadly.

Bambi sniffed at what Owl had mistaken for a tree.

"Owl—I think you must need spectacles!" chuckled Bambi. "This is ivy—not a tree. Your tower is covered by ivy!"

"How silly I am!" chuckled Owl. "You would think that a wise old bird like me would have realized it was ivy, and not a tree. Ivy does like to creep up things as it grows, and that is just what has happened to my tower. My tower is still here, but it is an ivy-covered tower now!"

Owl flew to the top of his tower, and managed to wriggle his way through the ivy, making himself a little doorway into his home.

"Thank you, Bambi," called Owl. "I will never forget the day when you were wiser than a wise owl!"

"I won't forget today, either!" said Bambi, proudly.

Dogs in the Fog

Kaa: "Was it hot where you spent your vacation?"
King Louie: "Terribly, and there were no trees! We took turns sitting in each other's shadow."

Pongo and Perdita had decided to take their puppies for a walk.

"It's time they had an airing. They're quite big enough to be taken out," said Pongo.

"Do you think we can manage them between us—all fifteen of them?" asked Perdita, a little worried. "They're such a handful, especially Pepper, and the other mischievous ones."

Pongo persuaded Perdita that everything would be all right, and with a good-bye *woof* to Roger (their master) and to Nan, who looked after them all, the seventeen dalmatians set off along the lane. They went through the town, and right across the park—and how the puppies enjoyed themselves! There were so many interesting things for them to see, so many sights and smells and sounds!

"Let's keep walking for ever!" woofed Penny. But Rolly said:

"I'm hungry, Mother. Let's go home and find something to eat!"

Perdita smiled. "We have been out for rather a long time, dear," she said to Pongo. "We must turn back now. Nan will be wondering what has happened to us."

Pongo agreed, and they all turned around to go back

across the park. It had been quite misty when they set out, and autumn mists can often fall thick and fast. By the time they had crossed the park the mist had turned into a fog—a gray, cloudy fog, through which the dogs could hardly see.

"Oh, Pongo! Do you think we'll be able to find our way home?" whispered Perdita to her husband.

Pongo assured her that his sense of smell was very good, and that he could track his way home blindfolded.

"But what about the puppies?" asked Perdita. "They are trailing behind us all over the place, and they haven't yet developed a sense of smell. How can they track their way home?"

"Now, Perdy, listen to me," he said. "Tell Pepper to hold my tail between his teeth—gently, mind—then tell Rolly to hold Pepper's tail, Patch to hold Rolly's tail, Penny to hold Patch's tail, Freckles to hold Penny's—and so on and so on—until all the pups are in a long line. Lucky shall be last of all, and you walk behind Lucky to make sure that no one lets go of the line, Perdy."

Soon the puppies were all in a long line behind Pongo, and Perdy walked behind them. Mouth to tail and mouth to tail, they were able to follow along behind Pongo, who sniffed his way home through the town. By now the fog was so thick that the puppies could not possibly have found their way without their brave, clever father.

"Keep going, Lucky!" Perdy encouraged the smallest puppy.

At last, Pongo reached his home. There, at the gate, were Roger and his wife with a flashlight.

"Oh, Pongo, we were just going to try to find you to help you home," cried Roger. "But I don't know how we could have found you—even with a light. This fog is so thick. I'm glad you're back and that all the puppies are safe. How clever of you to make them march in a line."

Roger counted the puppies, and was delighted to find that all fifteen were there. He shut the gate behind Perdy, and took all the pets indoors where a warm cozy fire was waiting to warm them. Nan gave each one a pat and a drink.

"Welcome home!" she smiled.

A Very Tiny Party

Fairy Tinker Bell lives in Never-Never Land with Peter Pan. Although she is rather a mischievous fairy, Peter is fond of her, and he agreed with Wendy when she said:

"It is Tinker Bell's birthday today, and it would be fun to plan a birthday party for her."

Tinker Bell liked the idea, too, and she flew off to Fairy Land to invite her fairy friends to the party. Wendy and Peter set to work preparing the party. Wendy made one small fairy cake for the birthday cake, and one sandwich, which she sliced into very tiny slices—small enough for fairies to eat. Peter found some colorful leaves to use as plates. Wendy placed the plates and food on a large flat stone that she had put in the center of a toadstool ring.

"The stone makes a fine table," said Wendy, "and the toadstools can be the fairy chairs."

"Now we have everything except cups," said Peter. "What can we use for fairy cups?"

"We could ask Tinker Bell to *magic* some with her fairy wand," said Wendy.

"But I want everything to be ready for Tinker Bell by the time she arrives with her guests," said Peter. "I don't want her to have to do any work for the party."

It was John, Wendy's brother, who came to their rescue.

"What about using *acorn* cups?" he said. "Michael and I will go and search for some."

The boys found plenty of acorns that had fallen from an oak tree, and they removed the little cup-shaped parts from the acorns and took them to Peter and Wendy. They were the perfect size for fairy cups. In fact the whole party was perfect.

"It's the best fairy party ever!" smiled Tinker Bell.

Paintbrush Tails

King Louie had found something in the jungle. It was large, cold and heavy. He couldn't carry it, so he bowled it all the way to his home. King Louie's home is an old, ruined temple, where he lives with all his monkeys.

The monkeys were eager to know what it was that King Louie had found. With sticks and stones they poked and banged until, at last, they found that the top of it came off. It was, in fact, a huge can of paint, and they soon discovered the white, sticky paint inside.

The can had fallen from a truck that had been passing along the jungle track.

"No one came back for it, so we'll keep it," said King Louie. "We'll paint our home! It will look nice all white, instead of dirty gray. We just have time to do it before the rainy season sets in."

"But what do we paint *with*?" asked a monkey. "Did some paintbrushes fall off the truck, too?"

"No," chuckled King Louie. "We'll have to use our *tails!*"

The monkeys and King Louie dipped their tails into the paint, and then what fun they had! They sang happily as they painted.

The ruin really looked quite nice by the time they had finished, but as for all their tails, well! For months after that anyone who made their way through the jungle was heard to remark:

"The monkeys in these parts all have WHITE tails! How very strange!"

147

The Football Watching Outfit

The merry March Hare had a ticket for the Wonderland football game. He was excited about it, and was up early on the morning of the game.

"I'll take a thermos of coffee with me," thought the March Hare. "It's nice to have a drink at halftime."

The March Hare opened his front door to fetch his pint of milk from the doorstep. He was only wearing his pajamas and bathrobe, and he shivered as the icy autumn wind whistled around him. The first frost had appeared that morning, and Wonderland had become a very cold place.

The March Hare shut his door and pulled his bathrobe around him tightly.

"I shall have to wrap up well," he decided.

Then he made his coffee, filled his thermos and hurried to find some warm clothes.

"I'll wear two undershirts and two pairs of pants," he said, "and three pairs of socks."

Then the funny hare pulled on some long trousers, and put a pair of short trousers on top of those. He pulled on his rubber boots, and he wore his floppy slippers over those.

"I'll wear a jacket, pullover, a waistcoat and my parka," said the March Hare. "I'll wear my raincoat over my parka, and I'll put on my wool hat, and my cap on top of that. And I mustn't forget my scarf."

He wrapped the gaily striped scarf, in his team colors, around his neck, and he wore a pair of gloves, with mittens on top of those!

"Now I'm *warm*," he said. "Not even the keenest, sharpest wind can reach me now. I'll keep warm all the way through the game, and I'll enjoy it because I won't have to worry about being cold."

The merry March Hare set off for the football game, with his thermos of coffee in one pocket and a hot water bottle in the other. He looked funny, and was so padded with clothes that he could only walk slowly. The Wonderland folks stopped to stare in surprise, and some of them couldn't help laughing at him. This did not bother the March Hare at all. He is such a merry fellow that nothing worries him!

149

The Before-Christmas Cake

The March Hare: "I don't have a windshield on my car."
Mad Hatter: "How do you keep the wind out of your face?"
The March Hare: "I ride on the bus!"

Flora, one of Princess Aurora's Fairy Godmothers, was making a cake for Christmas. She was working busily with dried fruits, nuts, sugar, flour, butter and all sorts of other good things.

"Isn't it early to be making a Christmas cake?" asked Fauna, the second Fairy Godmother.

"No," replied Flora. "It's wise to make a Christmas cake early, so that it can become sweeter, nuttier, fruitier and tastier by the time Christmas comes. Once it is cooked, I shall put it away in a tin, and put candies and icing on it when Christmas is near."

"Ooh, it sounds delicious," said Merryweather, the third Fairy Godmother. "Couldn't we have a little taste before you put it away?"

Merryweather is the greediest Godmother. She is plump, and always seems to be hungry.

"No," said Flora. "If I cut the cake, it will be spoiled for Christmas."

150

"Then couldn't we just have a taste of the mixture before you cook it?" asked Merryweather.

"No," said Flora. "The cake will only be small if you eat some of the mixture, but you may eat what is left in the mixing bowl, after I have put the mixture in the baking tin."

Merryweather cheered up, but she was disappointed when she saw that there was only a little mixture left in the bowl. Flora decided to cheer her up.

"There is a little dried fruit left over from my Christmas cake, and a few nuts," Flora said. "I'll put them into the sponge mixture that I've prepared for today's cake, as a special treat."

Flora put the leftover things into the sponge mixture and cooked it in the oven, with the Christmas cake. The sponge cake was ready to come out of the oven before the big Christmas cake, and Flora put it on a tray to cool. By teatime it was ready. Flora and Fauna each had a slice, and Merryweather had several!

"What an unusual cake," said Fauna. "We must think of a special name for it."

"I think it should be called Before-Christmas cake," laughed Merryweather, and the other Fairy Godmothers agreed!

151

A Friend for O'Malley

27
November

Donald: "Do men like talkative women or the other kind?"
Mickey: "What other kind?"

Thomas O'Malley was once an alley cat who roamed the streets, without a home of his own. In the summertime he enjoyed this way of life, but when the November evenings arrived he wished he had somewhere warm to sleep.

One damp, dreary night O'Malley found the very place! It was a roadside hut that belonged to old Bill, the nightwatchman. On this particular evening old Bill had set up his hut near a partly finished building. He had been paid to watch the building all night—to make sure no one came along to do any damage or steal any of the bricks.

Old Bill had lit himself a fire not far from his hut, and there he could make himself a hot, milky drink, or cook himself some sausages. It was the smell of the sausages sizzling that had first brought O'Malley to the hut.

"Hello, young fella!" said Bill to O'Malley. "You look as cold as I feel. Come and sit on this rug. You can have some of my milk, and a piece of sausage. With something warm inside your tummy, and a cozy fire beside you—you'll be warm in no time!"

152

How kind old Bill was, and how glad O'Malley was to have found such a good friend! He spent every night with old Bill, after that—all through the winter.

Only one thing worried O'Malley.

"I wish I could repay old Bill for his kindness," he thought. "He is so good to me, and I don't seem to be able to do anything for him."

Soon after that O'Malley had his chance, for old Bill said:

"Could you do something for me, young fella? Could you chase those noisy rats away from the building site?"

The workmen on the site often left scraps of food about from their lunches, and in the evenings the rats came to gobble up those crumbs. The rats made such a noise that it disturbed old Bill.

"I don't want to listen to scampering and scratching all night," said old Bill. "Off you go, fella! Send the rats away!"

O'Malley tore around the building site, sending the rats scurrying away to their homes.

Every evening after that, O'Malley did his rat-chasing job before settling down by Bill's fire, and old Bill was pleased with him.

"Now we can help each other!" smiled Bill. "That's what friends are for, isn't it?"

153

White Rabbit's Special Clock

The White Rabbit came rushing through Wonderland at great speed.

"I'm late!" he gasped. "I'm late for a very important appointment! And what's even worse—I don't know *how* late I am!"

The White Rabbit, you see, had lost his watch! It is a big one that hangs on a chain. The chain had broken, and the watch had fallen into the long grass somewhere. The White Rabbit would search for it later, after his important appointment. The appointment was tea with the Mad Hatter—not that it was important to the Mad Hatter! He is such a mad fellow that he wouldn't really notice which guests had turned up and which hadn't. The appointment was only important to the White Rabbit, who was very hungry, and wanted some tea!

"If I'm too late for the party, there will be no tea left," he sighed. "I know! I'll pick a dandelion clock—that will tell me what the time is."

He picked a dandelion that had gone to seed and began blowing the white, fluffy seeds into the air. *One—two—three—four* puffs, and all the seeds were gone.

"That means it is four o'clock," said the White Rabbit. "I'm too late for the Mad Hatter's tea party. That started at three o'clock!"

"Don't worry, White Rabbit," said a kind voice, nearby.

The White Rabbit looked around, and saw Alice, who had found a sunny spot to spread out her picnic tea.

"I've plenty of tea here for both of us, White Rabbit, if you would like to share my picnic," said Alice.

So the lucky White Rabbit had some tea after all!

Brer Fox and the Mole

29
November

Late one evening, when Brer Fox was prowling about, he saw a mole pop up out of the ground.

"You're only little," he told the mole. "I'm bigger, and I'm going to chase you."

Brer Fox started to chase the mole. The mole couldn't run fast, so he decided to hide. He began to dig a tunnel under the ground. He was a fast digger, and he managed to burrow his way down into the earth and out of Brer Fox's reach. Brer Fox could have dug down after the mole, but he wanted to *chase* and to *tease*. He was so cross that he stamped one of his paws. He stamped it down on to a hard, jagged piece of rock!

"Oh dear!" wailed Brer Fox. "This has happened just when I was about to dig a nice deep hole to keep me cozy during the cold months. Now my paw is hurt too badly for me to do any digging!"

The mole popped out of his tunnel.

"If you promise not to chase me, I'll fetch my relations and we'll dig a hole deep enough for your den."

Brer Fox made his promise, and the mole and his relations were soon at work. At last they had dug a hole big enough for Brer Fox.

"You see, even *little* folks can be useful at times," said the mole. "So don't you go around bullying little creatures any more."

"No," said Brer Fox.

He climbed into his den to wait for his paw to heal.

"I'll try to be good," he said.

Do you think he really will?

The Little Blue Van

It was a peaceful day. Everyone was behaving in an orderly fashion. No one was exceeding the speed limit, nor was anyone parking where they shouldn't be.

This was Goofy's first day as a traffic policeman, and he'd never felt happier.

A blue van approached Goofy, driven very carefully. On the side of it was written 'Little Mouse Convention'. Goofy frowned. There was something wrong. Goofy's frown deepened. He scratched his head. "Sheesh!" he gasped. "There's no one driving it!"

Yet the turn-sign flashed as the van turned left. The horn honked as a dog darted out in front of the van. It even slowed down for an old lady.

Goofy grabbed the nearest passerby, who happened to be Mickey Mouse. "Mickey! Quickly!" yelled Goofy. "Let's chase that blue van. There's no one at the wheel!"

Mickey waved down a two-seater bicycle, and he and Goofy leaped on to it. "Stop that van!" yelled Goofy.

"Save your breath and keep pedaling," advised Mickey.

"It might be an invisible man," gasped Goofy as the little blue van slowed down. CLUNK! The blue van had slowed down so quickly that the bicycle had crashed into the back of it! Goofy picked himself up and loped over to look at the van.

There was definitely NO ONE driving it! But just at that moment the van drew away again, nearly running over Goofy's big toe.

"Uh! Hey, blue van! Stop! I'm a policeman, and you shouldn't be on the road without a driver!" yelled Goofy

The little blue van slowed down and stopped.

By now quite a crowd of Disney folk had gathered to see the van without a driver. Taking a deep breath, Goofy opened the door and peered inside. And this is what he saw: Roquefort the mouse working the pedals, the Dormouse working the turn-sign and horn and keeping a lookout from the dashboard, and Gus and Jaq, the mice, working the steering wheel between them.

"We're going to the 'Little Mouse Convention'," squeaked the foursome.

"Uh!" gaped Goofy.

"Why wasn't *I* invited?" complained Mickey.

"Hop in!" grinned the Dormouse. "You can be our guest speaker!"